THE X FILES™

FIGHT THE FUTURE

ALSO PUBLISHED BY HARPERPRISM

The Making of The X-Files
Adapted for Young Readers

The X-Files *Scrapbook*

THE X FILES™

FIGHT THE FUTURE

CHRIS CARTER

ADAPTED FOR YOUNG READERS BY

ELIZABETH HAND

HarperPrism

A Division of HarperCollinsPublishers

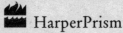

HarperPrism

A Division of HarperCollins*Publishers*
10 East 53rd Street, New York, NY 10022-5299

This is a work of fiction. The characters, incidents, and
dialogues are products of the author's imagination and are not to
be construed as real. Any resemblance to actual events or
persons, living or dead, is entirely coincidental.

ISBN 0-06-105934-X

Cover design © 1998 by Hamagami/Carroll & Associates
Cover artwork courtesy of and © 1998 by Twentieth Century
Fox Film Corporation

First printing: July 1998

Printed in the United States of America

Visit HarperPrism on the World Wide Web at
http://www.harperprism.com

❖ 10 9 8 7 6 5 4 3 2 1

PROLOGUE

NORTH TEXAS, 3500 B.C.

The desolated landscape stretches from horizon to horizon, all snow and ice and vast gray sky. In the distance two tiny figures appear, running desperately. They are manlike, with matted hair and coarse features, their bodies hidden beneath rough garments made of leather. They run across the white waste land, bodies bent as if they are scanning the ground underfoot for prints. The trail they seem to follow leads to a crevice, a triangular opening between slabs of ice and collapsed stone. At the mouth of the cave the prints disappear. One of the primitive men stoops to peer inside. They enter the cave.

Inside, the cave walls spiral. They are ribbed with ice that glistens faintly. The first primitive lights his torch. As he holds it up, his companion grabs his arm and points to where the cave twists a few yards ahead of them. There a soft patch of virgin snow bears the imprint of what they have been following. The torch sputters, and as though in reply a distinct scrabbling echoes back to them from the darkness ahead. The two men move quickly now. Ahead the cave splits into two tunnels. Without speaking, the two men each choose a different fork in the tunnel.

The first primitive moves quickly through the tunnel. At the far end he finds an opening barely wide enough for a man to squeeze through. He thrusts his torch into the opening, twisting it back and forth. He propels himself through the hole and drops into the next chamber.

It takes a moment to catch his breath. When he does, he raises the torch and peers around. He is in a roughly circular cavern perhaps thirty feet across, its walls shimmering ice nicked here and there by rocky outcroppings. One of these is larger than the rest. Gazing at it, the primitive frowns, then steps toward it.

Inches away from the outcropping he halts and reaches to touch what he sees—the body of another man, clad in furs and leather, a skin of ice encasing him from head to foot. Before he can reach it something strikes him from behind.

With a cry the primitive falls, the torch hurling

from him to drop sputtering to the floor. He curls into a ball, one hand clenched against his chest with the knife pointing outward; but something is already there, claws tearing at his clothes, shredding the thick protective layers of fur and stiff leather as though they were dry grass. The primitive cries out again. He rolls to one side, shoving his elbow into the creature's face, and strikes blindly and desperately with his knife. It shrieks; he feels something warm and wet spurt onto his hand. With a groan the primitive pulls away, staggering to the wall. He hears it thrashing in the darkness at his feet.

The primitive roars and strikes at it again, feels his knife shear through its skin. But there is no reassuring bite of bone and muscle beneath his hand; it is as though his knife is mired in the body. With a grunt the primitive yanks his knife back.

Too fast. The next instant he loses his balance and falls, and the thing is on him, its claws tearing at his thighs. His knife skids across the floor. Before he can reach for it a shadow fills the chamber. The cave seems to spin as light radiates everywhere, finally coming together into the torch held high by the second primitive, who has just appeared in the chamber. The creature looks up. The second primitive raises a knife and with a cry drives it into the creature.

A deafening shriek as the thing sprawls backward. A moment and the primitive is upon it, driving the knife into it again and again, as it tries to escape. With shocking strength and speed the creature throws the primitive to the cave floor.

Dazed, the primitive comes to his feet poised to attack. He pauses, gasping for breath, and gazes down at his fallen companion. Blood soaks his garments, and his eyes are already clouded. He is dead. The primitive turns away, searching for his enemy. His eyes dart as he moves through the cave. In a nearby chamber he comes upon the fallen body of his enemy. Warily he approaches, waving the torch at the creature's head. Slowly its eyes open. For a brief moment the gaze of the hunter and the hunted meet.

The primitive raises his knife to strike the final blow. Before his arm drops the creature swiftly attacks. In one motion the primitive drops the torch and with his other hand brings his knife forward, so that it slides through the creature's upper body. He withdraws it and stabs again, harder this time, while the creature writhes and the cavern echoes with its cries; strikes it until it lies motionless upon the floor.

The primitive draws back, breathing hard. In front of him his prey lies dead. Something black oozes from the creature's wounds. In the torchlight it seems to thicken and pool. As he stares at it, the primitive frowns.

There is a tiny crack in the cavern floor. The black oily substance moves toward it. Not naturally, like water seeking its level, but like something alive. He watches, mesmerized, as the oil fills the crevice almost to overflowing, then disappears down the crack. It is several moments before he notices something else.

Across his chest are dark blots where the creature's blood has spattered him. The primitive's gaze is drawn to a single oily drop. He stares at it, brows furrowing. His expression changes from curiosity to horror. There are drops of black ooze everywhere upon him, crawling up his torso, along his arms, across the tops of his thighs, and over his chest. He grunts and begins brushing at them, but they will not move. He opens his mouth to scream but no sound comes out.

# CHAPTER 1

Without warning a boy plunged through the roof of the cave.

"Stevie? Hey, Stevie—you okay?" a voice called from the opening above him. Three other boys stood there, peering nervously through the hole. For the last few days they'd been building a fort there, digging at the ground. Behind them, sun glared off the hard-baked earth. Miles to the east, the glittering contours of the Dallas skyline reared against the horizon. In the near-distance stretched a housing development, identical buildings scattered across a dun-colored landscape.

On the floor of the cave, Stevie lay winded. "I

7

got—I got—I got the wind knocked out of me," he gasped at last.

Relieved laughter. Jason's and Chuck's faces appeared alongside Jeremy's. "Looks like you were right, Stevie," Jason called down. "Looks like a cave or something."

Jeremy jostled the other boys, trying to get a better view. "What's down there, Stevie? Anything?"

Slowly Stevie got to his feet. He took a few unsteady steps. In the darkness something glistened, something round and smooth and roughly the size of a soccer ball. He picked it up and tilted it very carefully, so that the light struck it and it seemed to glow in his hands.

"Stevie?" Jeremy called again. "C'mon, what'd you find?"

"Human skull," breathed Stevie. "It's a human *skull!*"

Jason whooped. "Toss it up here, dude!"

Stevie shook his head. "No *way*, buttwipe. It's mine." He stood, looking around in amazement. "Holy cow. Anyways, there's bones all over the place down here."

He took a few steps back toward the pool of sunlight. He looked down, and saw that he was standing in some kind of oil slick. When he tried pulling his foot up, the ground sucked at the sole of his sneaker.

And then he saw that the oil was everywhere, not just beneath his feet, but seeping up from cracks in the rock. And it was *moving*. Moving toward *him*. Black oil oozed up beneath his foot and wriggled down and into his sneaker. The skull fell from his hands and bounced across the stony floor as he tugged at his shorts and stared at the exposed skin of his leg.

Beneath the flesh something moved; a writhing thing as long as his finger. Only now there was more than one, there were dozens of them, all burrowing under his skin and moving upward. And there was something else, something just as frightening: where the black oil passed, his limbs were left feeling numb and frozen. Paralyzed.

"Stevie?" Jeremy stared down into the darkness. "Hey, Stevie?"

Stevie grunted but did not look up at him. Jeremy watched, unsure whether this was some kind of joke. "Stevie, you better not—"

"Stevie?" the other boys chimed in. "You okay?"

Stevie was definitely not okay. As they stared, Stevie's head fell backward so that he seemed to stare straight up at them, and in the glaring desert light they could see his eyes first filling with darkness and then turning completely, unnaturally black.

"Hey, man," whispered Jason. "Let's get outta here."

"Wait," said Jeremy. "We should help him—"

Jason and Chuck pulled him away. Jeremy went with them reluctantly, his footsteps echoing loudly against the dusty ground.

Sirens wailed counterpoint to the rush of wind over the plain. In the housing development doors slammed as people began to file onto their front steps a few at a time.

The fire engines were already there. Two men in full rescue mode jumped from the hook-and-ladder vehicle, disengaged a ladder, and hurried toward the hole left by the boys. Several other men followed them as the captain pulled up in his car and hopped out, radio in hand.

"This is Captain Miles Cooles," he recited. "We've got a rescue situation in progress."

He stepped toward the hole. The three lead firemen had already slung the ladder down there, and two of them quickly stepped down it. Their helmets gleamed in the sunlight, then winked from view as they reached the bottom and stepped away from the ladder.

"What you got down there, T.C.?" Cooles yelled after him. There was no response.

Outside, the sun beat down on the growing circle of parents and children that had gathered. Captain Cooles stood silently, his weathered face taut with concern as he stared at the hole. After a moment he sent two more men down.

Cooles glanced up sharply, momentarily distracted from his urgent attempts to reach the men in the cave. A low ominous *whomp whomp* echoed through the air, as a helicopter mysteriously appeared out of the sunset. Around him more and more people were slowly appearing, parents and children all staring at the western horizon. Faster than seemed possible the helicopter approached the huddled group, banked sharply and then hovered above them. People clapped their palms over their ears and shaded their eyes as clouds of dust rose and the unmarked copter landed gently on the parched earth.

What the heck? thought Cooles. The helicopter's side door flew open, and five figures jumped out. Swathed in white Hazardous Materials suits, their faces hidden behind heavy masks, they carried a gleaming metal litter capped by a translucent plastic bubble, like an immense beetle shell. They headed immediately for the hole. Cooles nodded and started after them, but before he had gone two paces another man got out of the helicopter, a tall gaunt figure in a white oxford-cloth shirt, his tie flapping in the propellers' backwash.

"Get those people back!" the man yelled, pointing to where the crowd was drifting curiously after the paramedics. A plastic tag around his neck identified him as Dr. Ben Bronschweig. "Get them out of here!"

Cooles nodded. He turned to the line of waiting firemen and shouted, "Move them all back! Now!" Then, hurrying to catch up with Bronschweig, he said, "I sent my men down after the boy. The report is that his eyes went black. That's the last I heard—"

Bronschweig ignored him and made a beeline for the hole. Already the figures were climbing back up the ladder, bearing the limp body of the young boy on the bubble litter. At the sight of this Bronschweig finally stopped, staring as the rescue crew bore it back toward the chopper. The crew followed, and as the gathered crowd watched in silence, the helicopter lifted back into the air, its blades sending billows of red dust like smoke across the plain. A minute later and it was only a black smudge against the sky.

Bronschweig walked toward the development, Captain Cooles close behind. In the near distance a line of unmarked heavy vehicles barreled along the highway, turning into the access road leading to the little rows of identical houses. Unmarked cargo vans and squat trucks were driven by blank-faced men in dark uniforms. At the front of this threatening caravan were two huge white tanker trucks, devoid of any logo or advertising, gleaming ominously in the dying sun. Bronschweig stopped, arms crossed on his chest, and watched them with a tense expression.

"What about my men?" Captain Cooles loomed angrily at the doctor's side, his face red. "I sent five men down there—"

Bronschweig turned and walked away without a word.

Cooles waved furiously back at the hole. "Did you hear what I said? I sent—"

Seeming not to hear him, Bronschweig walked toward the approaching trucks. A few of them had parked in a line in the cul-de-sac. Official-looking personnel were already pulling tents and tent poles, satellite dishes, banks of electric lights and monitoring equipment from them. The townspeople stared in bewilderment as the first of many refrigeration units were yanked from the backs of trucks and moved toward the hole. Drivers continued maneuvering the huge trucks, efficiently forming a barrier blocking the scene of action from the crowd's view.

Bronschweig disappeared into the melee. When he reached the tanker trucks he ducked between them and withdrew a cell phone. His face tight, he punched in a number, waited and then spoke.

"Sir? The impossible scenario we hadn't planned for?" He listened for a moment, then replied, "Well, we better come up with a plan."

CHAPTER 2

FEDERAL BUILDING,
DALLAS, TEXAS

One week later, on a rooftop in Dallas, fifteen agents in dark windbreakers printed with the letters FBI watched as another helicopter hovered above them. When the chopper touched down the side door was flung open, and a single man emerged: Special Agent-in-Charge Darius Michaud.

One of the agents met him, cell phone in hand. "We've evacuated the building and been through it bottom to top. No trace of an explosive device, or anything resembling one."

Michaud looked at him. "Have you taken the dogs through?"

The agent nodded. "Yes, sir."

"Well, take them through again."

"Yes, sir," he replied.

Michaud turned and scanned the Dallas skyline. Suddenly he stiffened. He stared to where a solitary figure emerged from a door on the neighboring roof: a slender form in a FBI windbreaker, a glint of sunlight on her shoulder-length red hair.

Michaud's hands clenched at the edge of the wall.

On the other rooftop, Special Agent Dana Scully jabbed at her cell phone.

"Mulder?" she said urgently into the phone. "It's me."

Mulder's voice echoed in her ear. "Where are you, Scully?"

"I'm on the roof."

"Did you find anything?"

"No, Mulder. I *haven't*."

"What's wrong, Scully?"

Scully shook her head impatiently. "I've just climbed twelve floors, I'm hot and thirsty and I'm wondering, to be honest, what I'm doing here."

"You're looking for a bomb," Mulder's unflappable voice replied.

Scully sighed. "I know that. But the threat was called in for the federal building across the street."

"I think they have that covered."

Scully took a deep breath and began, "Mulder, when a terrorist bomb threat is called in, the logical purpose of providing this information is to allow us to *find the bomb*. The rational object of terrorism is to provide terror. If you'd study the statistics, you'd find a model behavioral pattern in virtually every case where a threat has turned up an explosive device—"

She paused, and drew the cell phone closer. "If we don't act in accordance with that data, Mulder—if you ignore it as we have done—the chances are great that if there actually *is* a bomb, we might not find it. Lives could be lost—"

She paused again and suddenly realized she'd been the only one talking for the last few minutes. "Mulder . . . ?"

"What happened to playing a hunch?"

Scully almost jumped out of her skin: the voice came not from her cell phone but from two feet away. There stood Fox Mulder. He cracked a sunflower seed between his teeth and stepped toward her.

"Jeez, Mulder!" Scully moaned.

"There's an element of surprise, Scully," said Mulder. "Random acts of unpredictability."

He popped another sunflower seed into his mouth. "If we fail to anticipate the unforeseen or expect the unexpected in a universe of unforeseen possibilities, we find ourselves at the mercy of anyone or anything that cannot be programmed, categorized, or easily referenced . . ."

He walked toward the edge of the building, turned to Scully and said, "What are we doing up here? It's hotter than heck."

"I know you're bored in this assignment," said Scully. "But unconventional thinking is only going to get you into trouble now."

"How's that?"

"You've got to quit looking for what isn't there. They've closed the X-Files, Mulder. There's procedure to be followed here. *Protocol.*"

Mulder nodded. "What do you say we call in a bomb threat for Houston," he suggested. "I think it's free beer night at the Astrodome."

Scully gave him a look, but it was no use. Sighing, she hurried past him up the stairs, took the last few steps until she stood at the top, and grabbed the doorknob. She twisted it, once, twice, and looked back at Mulder.

"Now what?" she demanded, her face grim.

Mulder's impish expression vanished. "It's locked?"

Scully wiggled the knob again. "So much for anticipating the unforeseen . . ."

She squinted up at the sun, then gazed at Mulder. Before she could say anything else he lunged past her, yanking her hand from the knob. He turned it, and the door opened easily.

"Had you." Scully smirked.

Mulder shook his head. "No, you didn't."

"Oh, yeah. Had you big time."

"No, you *didn't*—"

She slid past him into the stairwell and headed for the freight elevator. She punched a button and waited for the doors to open.

"Sure did," she said, still grinning. "I saw your face, Mulder. There was a moment of panic."

Mulder stood beside her as the elevator dropped. "Panic? Have you ever seen me panic, Scully?"

The elevator drew to a halt. The doors opened onto a busy lobby filled with men and women in business suits, deliverymen, and a bored-looking security guard.

"I just did," Scully said as she walked into the lobby. Before her a group of schoolchildren parted, staring excitedly at her FBI jacket. "You're buying."

"When I panic, I make this face," said Mulder, staring at her completely deadpan.

Scully glanced at him. "Yeah, that's the face you made."

Mulder followed her. "All right," he said.

Scully stood with her arms crossed and stared pointedly at a door with a sign that read SNACKS/BEVERAGES. Mulder dug in his pocket, fishing for change as he asked, "What'll it be? Coke, Pepsi? A saline IV?"

"Something sweet."

Mulder rolled his eyes and headed for the lounge. He sorted through a handful of change as someone elbowed by him on his way out of the vending room. A tall man in a blue vendor's uniform, with short black hair. He looked casually over at Mulder. Mulder glanced back, then hurried inside to catch the door before it closed.

Inside the windowless room Mulder went straight to a large, brightly lit soft drink machine. One by one he plunked the coins through the slot. Then he hit a button, leaned back on his heels, and—

Nothing.

"Oh, come *on*," groaned Mulder. He beat his fist against the front of the machine—still nothing—and finally rummaged through his pocket for more change. Slid it into the machine—nothing.

"*Darn* it."

He stared at the machine, then pounded it with both fists.

Nothing.

Mulder moved around to the back of the machine. He crouched and looked behind it, frowning.

The machine wasn't plugged in.

He picked up the plug, stared at it with growing comprehension and horror.

In the lobby, Scully waited impatiently, wondering what was taking Mulder so long. She was thirsty.

The door wouldn't open.

"No." Mulder jiggled the knob, but there was no doubt. He was locked in.

He pulled out his cell phone and punched in a number. A moment later Scully answered.

"Scully."

Mulder took a deep breath. "Scully, I found the bomb."

In the lobby, Scully rolled her eyes. "You're funny, Mulder."

"I'm in the vending room."

She headed for the vending room. When she heard faint pounding she stopped in front of a door that said SNACKS/BEVERAGES.

"Is that you pounding?" she asked.

On the other side, Mulder pounded even harder. "Scully, get someone to open this door."

Scully shook her head. "Nice try, Mulder."

Mulder started pulling at the front of the soda machine. "Scully, listen to me. The bomb is in the Coke machine. You've got about fourteen minutes to get this building evacuated.

"Mulder?" She breathed into the cell phone. "Tell me this is a joke."

Mulder's voice echoed in her ear. "Thirteen fifty-nine, thirteen fifty-eight, thirteen fifty-seven . . ."

Scully bent to examine the keyhole. It had been soldered over—recent work.

". . . thirteen fifty-six . . . Do you see a pattern emerging here, Scully?"

"Hang on," said Scully. "I'm gonna get you out of there."

Inside the vending room, Mulder's phone went dead. He squatted in front of the soda machine. Inside was a battery of circuit boards and wires, digital readouts and row after row of clear plastic canisters filled with fluid hooked up to what had to be explosives. In the middle of all this a blinking LED display registered the countdown. Mulder stared at it, and thought, *It's gonna take an expert a lot longer than thirteen minutes to figure out where to even start on this. . . .*

In the lobby Scully ran up to the security desk.

"I need this building evacuated and cleared out in ten minutes!" She yelled at the security chief. "I need you to get on the phone and tell the fire department to block off the city center in a one-mile radius around the building—"

The security chief gaped. "In *ten minutes?*"

"DON'T THINK!" shouted Scully. "JUST PICK UP THE PHONE AND MAKE IT HAPPEN!"

But people in the lobby were already running out and she was gone before he could protest, already dialing another number on her phone.

"This is Special Agent Dana Scully. I need to speak to SAC Michaud. He's got the wrong building—"

She stopped beside the front revolving doors. Vans and cars were suddenly screeching up to the curb. Agents in FBI windbreakers ran from the unmarked vehicles, Darius Michaud among them.

"Where is it?" he demanded. Around them workers ran out of the building.

"Mulder found it in a vending machine. He's locked in with it."

Michaud looked over his shoulder and yelled at an agent. "Get Kesey with the torch! It's in the vending room."

He looked back at Scully. "Take me there," he commanded.

"This way—"

• • •

In the windowless room Mulder stared at the explosives and the LED display.

7:00

His cell phone rang, startling him, and he answered it. "Scully? You know that face I was making—I'm making it now."

"Mulder," ordered Scully. "Move away from the door. We're coming through it—"

He backed away as a gas plasma torch began to cut through the metal door. Mulder heard a series of thumps and a voice yelling *"Go!"* The door fell inward and crashed to the floor.

Scully came in with Michaud and three other technicians—bomb techs. They headed for the soda machine.

4:07

Mulder shook his head. "Tell me that's just soda pop in those canisters."

"No," said Michaud. "It's what it looks like. A big bomb—ten gallons of astrolite."

For a moment Michaud studied the bomb. Then he commanded, "Okay. Get everybody out of here and clear the building."

Mulder frowned. "Somebody's got to stay here with you—"

"I gave you an order," Michaud snapped. "Now get out of here and evacuate the area."

"Can you defuse it?" asked Scully.

"I think so." Michaud took a pair of wire clippers from his tool box. The other agents quickly left the room.

"You've got about four minutes to find out if you're wrong," said Mulder.

Michaud turned on him. "Did you hear what I said?"

"Let's go, Mulder," Scully murmured. "Come on."

She started out the door. Mulder remained for a moment longer, staring at Michaud.

But the other man's attention was focused on the bomb. Finally Mulder turned and followed Scully into the corridor. In the room behind him Michaud set the wire clippers carefully on his knee but did nothing else; only sat staring at the bomb. Just staring.

In the lobby, everyone had been evacuated. A running FBI agent yelled out, "All clear." Scully and Mulder raced out the revolving doors. A car waited for them a few yards away. Abruptly Mulder stopped and stared at the building.

"What are you doing?" Scully cried. "Mulder?"

Mulder whispered, "Something's wrong . . ."

Scully hurried to his side. *Mulder?*

"Something's not right," Mulder said again. Scully shook her head and grabbed his arm.

"Mulder! Get in the car! There's no time, Mulder!"

She pulled him after her, heading for the car. Mulder twisted to stare over his shoulder.

"Michaud . . ." he said.

In the vending room, Michaud had replaced the wire clippers and shut his tool chest. Now he was sitting on it, his eyes fixed on the LED display.

:30

He watched as the seconds disappeared, yet still did nothing. Finally he let his head drop forward against his chest.

Outside the sun beat heedlessly upon the nearly empty plaza.

"Mulder!" Scully shouted. "Get in!"

Mulder slid into the backseat, Scully into the front, and the car peeled off. They turned to gaze out the rear window, watching as the building receded.

And suddenly it exploded. The entire structure was consumed by a ball of flame that ripped up from the bottom floor. Smoke surged outward along with steel girders and waves of broken glass. The air thundered as the building collapsed.

The bomb's impact traveled through the air and pushed the agents' car across the plaza where it slammed against a parked car. Their car lifted up in the back and then slammed back down. All around them other cars did the same. There was a sharp *crack*, and the rear window collapsed, showering Mulder and Scully with broken glass.

"You okay?" bellowed the agent from the front seat.

"I-I think so," Scully gasped.

Mulder shook his head. He looked at Scully.

"Next time, *you're* buying," he said darkly.

CHAPTER 3

The sign on the door read OFFICE OF PROFESSIONAL REVIEW. Inside, Agent Scully shifted nervously in her chair and tried to focus on what was being said.

"In light of Waco and Ruby Ridge . . ."

This review was important, far too important for Mulder to be late. Scully herself had barely made it here on time. In front of her, six assistant directors sat at a long table. At the center of the conference table Assistant Director Jana Cassidy was talking.

". . . for the catastrophic destruction of public property and the loss of life due to terrorist activities . . ."

At the end of the row, Assistant Director Walter Skinner cast Scully a sad look. Over the years Skinner had spent a lot of time with Agents Mulder and Scully, who reported directly to him. When he could get away with it, he'd tried to help Mulder and Scully.

"Many details are still unclear," said Jana Cassidy. "Some agents' reports have not been filed, or have come in sketchy, without a satisfactory accounting of the events that led to the destruction in Dallas. But we're under some pressure to give an accurate picture of what happened to the Attorney General, so she can issue a public statement."

And then Scully heard what she'd been waiting for: a familiar footstep. She turned to see Mulder enter the room. Jana Cassidy glared sternly at the two of them.

"We know now that five people died in the explosion," said Cassidy. "Special Agent-in-Charge Darius Michaud, who was trying to defuse the bomb that had been hidden inside a vending machine. Three firemen from Dallas, and a young boy."

Mulder looked quickly at Scully.

"Excuse me—" said Mulder. "The firemen and the boy—they were in the building?"

"Agent Mulder, since you weren't able to be on time for this meeting, I'm going to ask you to step back outside, so that we can get Agent Scully's version of the facts. So that she won't have to be paid the same disrespect that you're showing the rest of us."

Mulder stared her down. "We were told the building was clear."

"You'll get your turn, Agent Mulder." Cassidy gestured at the door. "Please step out."

Mulder swallowed and looked at the table. The only sympathetic face he found was Skinner's, but Skinner's sympathy was tempered with a warning. Mulder turned to Cassidy and went on, "It does say there in your paperwork that Agent Scully and I were the ones who found the bomb . . ."

Cassidy sternly waved him off. "Thank you, Agent Mulder. We'll call you back in shortly."

Defeated, Mulder left the room. A moment later, Walter Skinner quietly excused himself and followed Mulder into the hallway.

He found the younger agent standing in front of a display case, staring broodingly at the marksmanship trophies inside.

"Sit down," said Skinner, indicating a beige couch. "It'll be a few minutes. They're still talking to Agent Scully."

Mulder plopped onto the couch, and Skinner joined him. "About what?"

"They're asking her for a narrative. They want to know why she was in the wrong building."

"She was with me."

Skinner shook his head. "You don't see what's going on, do you?" he said softly. "There's forty million dollars in damage to the city of Dallas. Lives have been lost. No suspects have been named. So the story being shaped is that *this could have been prevented*. That the FBI didn't do its job."

"And they want to blame us?"

"Agent Mulder, we both know that if you and Agent Scully hadn't taken the initiative to search the adjacent building, we could have multiplied those fatalities by a hundred—"

"But it's not the lives we saved." Mulder paused, savoring the irony. "It's the lives we didn't."

"If it looks bad, it's bad for the FBI."

Mulder's hand clenched. "If they want someone to blame, they can blame me. Agent Scully doesn't deserve this."

"She's in there right now saying the same thing about you."

Mulder shook his head. "I breached protocol. I broke contact with the SAC. . . ."

He paused, remembering Michaud's drawn face as he stared at the explosive-rigged vending machine. "I-I ignored a primary tactical rule and left him alone with the device . . ."

"Agent Scully says it was she who ordered you out of the building. That you wanted to go back—"

"Look, she was—"

Before he could go on, the door opened. The two men looked up to see Scully exiting. The look she gave Mulder told him that, whatever had happened inside the Professional Review Office, it hadn't gone well. She took a deep breath, then stepped briskly to where the men sat.

"They've asked for you, sir," she said, indicating Skinner.

Skinner gave one last look at Mulder. Then he stood and, thanking Scully, returned to the review. Mulder stared at Scully and after a moment said, "Whatever you told them in there, you don't have to protect me."

"All I told them was the truth."

"They're trying to divide us on this, Scully." Mulder's voice rose. "We can't let them."

For the first time Scully gazed directly at her partner. "They *have* divided us, Mulder. They're splitting us up."

On the couch Mulder stared back at her, not

understanding. Finally he said, "What? What are you talking about?"

"I meet with OPR day after tomorrow for remediation and reassignment."

Mulder looked stricken. "Why?"

"I think you must have an idea. They cited a history of problems relating back to 1993."

"But they were the ones who put us together—" Mulder protested.

"Because they wanted me to invalidate your work," Scully interrupted. "Your investigations into the paranormal. But I think this goes deeper than that . . ."

"This isn't about you, Scully." Mulder stared at her pleadingly. "They're doing this to *me*—"

"*They're* not doing this, Mulder." Scully looked away, avoiding his gaze. "I left behind a career in medicine because I thought I might make a difference at the FBI. When they recruited me, they told me that women made up nine percent of the Bureau. I felt that was not an impediment, but an opportunity to distinguish myself.

"But it hasn't turned out that way. And now, even if I were to be transferred to Omaha, or Wichita, or some other field office where I'm sure I could rise—it just doesn't hold the interest for me it once did. Not after what I've seen and done."

She fell silent. Mulder looked at her in disbelief. "You're . . . quitting?"

Scully shrugged. "There's really no reason for me to stay anymore. Maybe you should ask yourself if your heart's still in it, too."

Behind them the door to the hearing room opened. Mulder looked up, his expression still stunned as he saw Walter Skinner gesturing to him.

"Agent Mulder. You're up."

Scully looked at him sadly. "I'm sorry," she said softly. "Good luck."

Like a doomed man, Mulder followed Skinner into the office.

CHAPTER 4

CASEY'S BAR,
WASHINGTON, D.C.

Mulder had never liked Casey's much, but now he'd been here since late afternoon, and the bartender was wondering if he was ever going to leave. The place was nearly empty, except for two or three people and another man staring at him from the end of the bar. An older gray-haired man, with a broad, weathered face and wearing an old rumpled suit. Mulder looked at him blearily, then turned back to the bartender.

"Another shot."

The bartender poured it. "So, what do you do?" she asked.

"What do I do?" Mulder looked up at her.

"I'm a key figure in an ongoing government charade. An annoyance to my superiors. A joke among my peers. They call me 'Spooky.' Spooky Mulder . . .

"Whose sister was abducted by aliens when he was a kid. Who now chases little green men with a badge and a gun, shouting to the heavens and anyone else who'll listen that the fix is in. That our government's hip to the truth and a part of the conspiracy. That the sky is falling, and when it hits it's gonna be the bomb blast of all time."

What a freak, the bartender thought. She quickly pulled back the shot she'd just poured.

"I think that just about does it, Spooky." She dumped the drink in the sink.

"Does what?"

"Looks like eighty-six is your lucky number."

"One is the loneliest number."

She shook her head. "Too bad. Closing time for you."

Mulder shrugged and slid off the stool. He walked unsteadily toward the back of the room, where a door opened onto an alley. He went outside, but before he could take another step a voice came from behind him.

"You on official FBI business?"

"*What?*" Mulder whirled around.

A figure emerged from the shadows: the same older man in a rumpled suit who'd been inside the bar.

"Do I know you?" asked Mulder.

"No. But I've been watching your career for a good while. Back when you were just a promising young agent. Before that . . ."

"You follow me out here for a reason?"

"Yeah. I did. My name's Kurtzweil. Dr. Alvin Kurtzweil."

Mulder frowned.

"Old friend of your father's." Kurtzweil smiled at Mulder's bewildered expression. "Back at the Department of State. We were what you might call fellow travelers, but his disenchantment outlasted mine."

"How'd you find me?" Mulder demanded. "You a reporter?"

Kurtzweil shook his head. "I'm a doctor, but I think I mentioned that."

"Who sent you?"

"I came on my own. After reading about the bombing in Dallas."

"Well, if you've got something to tell me, you've got as long as it takes for me to hail a cab," said Mulder. He started down the alley.

Kurtzweil grabbed his arm. "They're going to pin

Dallas on you, Agent Mulder. But there was nothing you could've done. Nothing *anyone* could've done to prevent that bomb from going off—

"Because the truth is something you'd never have guessed. Never even have predicted."

Mulder pulled away and stormed down the sidewalk. Kurtzweil followed him doggedly. "And what's that?" Mulder snapped.

"SAC Darius Michaud never tried or intended to defuse the bomb."

Mulder looked at him in disgust. "Sure. He just let it explode."

Kurtzweil tugged at his raincoat. "What's the question nobody's asking? Why *that* building? Why not the federal building?"

"The federal building was too well guarded—"

"*No.*" Mulder stepped into the street, raising his hand to hail a cab. "They put the bomb in the building across the street because it *did* have federal offices. The Federal Emergency Management Agency had a provisional medical quarantine office there. Which is where the bodies were found. But *that's* the thing—"

The taxi pulled over. Kurtzweil followed Mulder to it. "—the thing you didn't know. That you'd never think to check."

Mulder was already pulling the door open.

Kurtzweil gazed at him challengingly and said, "Those people were already dead."

Mulder blinked. "Before the bomb went off?"

"That's what I'm saying."

Mulder stared at him. He shook his head. "Michaud was a twenty-two-year veteran of the Bureau—"

"Michaud was a patriot. The men he's loyal to know their way around Dallas. They blew away that building to hide something. Maybe something even they couldn't predict."

"You're saying they destroyed an entire building to hide the bodies of three firemen . . . ?"

"*And* one little boy."

Mulder got into the cab and slammed the door. He looked at the driver. "Take me to Arlington." He rolled down the window and stared up at Kurtzweil.

"I think you're full of it," he said.

"Do you?" Kurtzweil asked evenly. He rapped the taxi's roof and stepped away, watching as it sped away. "Do you really, Agent Mulder?" he repeated to himself thoughtfully.

Inside the cab, Mulder leaned forward. "I changed my mind," he said to the driver. "I want to go to Georgetown."

AGENT DANA SCULLY'S APARTMENT

Scully lay in bed, staring at the ceiling. She listened as the rain battered the walls of her apartment, and then she heard something else. She sat bolt upright, cocking her head.

Someone was pounding at the door. Scully glanced at her bedside clock. 3:17. She grabbed her bathrobe and hurried into the living room. She peeked through the peephole.

Mulder stood there, his clothes wet and hair disheveled. He looked strangely, even disturbingly, alert.

"I wake you?" he asked.

Scully shook her head. "No."

"Why not?" Mulder breezed past her into the apartment. "It's three A.M.—"

She closed the door and stared at him in disbelief. "Are you *drunk*, Mulder?"

"I was until about twenty minutes ago."

Scully crossed her arms against her chest. "Is that before or after you got the idea to come here?"

Mulder looked puzzled. "What are you implying, Scully?"

"I thought you may have gotten drunk and decided to come here to talk me out of quitting."

"Is that what you'd like me to do?"

Scully shut her eyes. Recalling how fifteen minutes ago, an hour ago, she had been thinking exactly that. After a moment she sighed. "Go home, Mulder. It's late."

He shook his head. "Get dressed, Scully."

"Mulder, what are you *doing?*"

"Just get dressed," he said. He couldn't hide the beginning of a grin, the slightest hint that something big was afoot. "I'll explain on the way."

CHAPTER 5

BLACKWOOD, TEXAS

Two unmarked helicopters swooped above the Texas flatlands, quiet-flight twin turbines humming. They flew at dangerously low altitude toward their destination: a large, ominously glowing dome. Only a few hundred yards away was a housing development and the hole where Stevie had fallen.

Now, several geodesic dome tents stretched over nearly the entire patch of ground. They were surrounded by long white cargo trucks and support vehicles: cars, vans, pickup trucks. Men in black fatigues walked around the domes, and other people in white Hazardous Material suits.

Overhead, the two choppers banked and slowly settled upon the ground. Dust devils spun up around them; tents billowed and tugged at their struts. An instant later one chopper's door swung open. A man stepped down and lit a cigarette.

"Sir?" The Cigarette-Smoking Man inhaled and looked at the uniformed man addressing him. "Dr. Bronschweig is waiting for you."

The Cigarette-Smoking Man regarded him through slit eyes. After a moment he nodded and followed the other man to the central dome.

"This way, sir." The man held open a vinyl flap, and the Cigarette-Smoking Man ducked beneath.

Inside, the dome was a maze of clear plastic tubing and vinyl walls separating one work area from another. Men and women worked at stainless steel tables, wearing Haz-Mat suits or surgical masks. There were refrigeration units everywhere. The Cigarette-Smoking Man put on a Haz-Mat suit and entered another work area.

Inside it was cold. Several metal gurneys were tucked beneath plastic sheathing. In the middle of it all a small mound of bare earth had been covered by a clear plastic cover, like a manhole cover: twelve inches thick, its transparent surface crisscrossed by heavy stainless steel bars. The walls of the earthen hole had been shored up by inserting a metal tube into the ground, big enough for a man to pass through. It was from this that Dr. Bronschweig appeared, wearing a Haz-Mat suit. He pushed aside the clear plastic hatch and stepped out.

The Cigarette-Smoking Man approached him and said, "You've got something to show me."

Dr. Bronschweig nodded. "Yes."

He pointed to the hatch. The Cigarette-Smoking Man slung himself down the hole, moving awkwardly in his suit as he went down the ladder. Dr. Bronschweig followed.

They were inside the cave. "We brought the atmosphere here back down to freezing in order to control its development," Dr. Bronschweig explained. "And that development is like nothing we've ever seen . . ."

The Cigarette-Smoking Man stood beside him, catching his breath. "Brought on by what?"

"Heat, I think. The coincident invasion of a host—the fireman—and an environment that raised his body temperature above 98.6."

He motioned the other man to follow him. At the other end of the cavern more plastic sheets hung from the ceiling. Dr. Bronschweig pushed them aside.

"Here—"

Behind the plastic was another gurney, different from the others. There was a body on it. A body covered with tubes and cords and wires that led to monitors lined up against the wall. The Cigarette-Smoking Man quietly stared down at its contents.

"This man's still alive," he said. He stared at the body before him. The skin was nearly transparent, a clear gray jelly of tissue and muscle. Its veins and capillaries were clearly visible, pulsing slightly.

Dr. Bronschweig shrugged. "Technically and biologically. But he'll never recover."

The Cigarette-Smoking Man shook his head. "How can this be?"

"The developing organism is using his life energy, digesting bone and tissue. We've just slowed the process." He shone a lamp directly on the fireman's face. Beneath the cheek, something moved.

The Cigarette-Smoking Man grimaced.

On the gurney, the body of the fireman shuddered. His chest heaved. Not as though he were breathing; as though something inside had moved and stretched. The Cigarette-Smoking Man stared, and as he did he saw a hand attached to what had to be an organism.

Then the dark shape *blinked*. Just once, very slowly.

It was an eye, a wakeful eye. Watching him.

Waiting.

The Cigarette-Smoking Man's mind worked frantically as he measured all the possibilities of what was before him; all the consequences . . .

"Do you want us to destroy this one, too?" Dr. Bronschweig was asking. "Before it gestates?"

The Cigarette-Smoking Man waited. "No," he said at last. "No . . . we need to try out the vaccine on it."

"And if it's unsuccessful?"

"Burn it. Like the others."

Dr. Bronschweig frowned. "This man's family will want to see the body laid to rest."

"Tell them he died trying to save the young boy's life. That he died heroically, like the other firemen."

"Of what?"

"They seemed to buy our story about the Hanta virus." The Cigarette-Smoking Man pursed his lips. "You'll make sure the families are taken care of financially, along with a sizable donation to the community. Maybe a small roadside memorial." Then he turned and left.

CHAPTER 6

BETHESDA NAVAL HOSPITAL

Inside, Walter Reed Hospital looked like any other hospital. But the few people Mulder and Scully passed wore navy uniforms and the shadowy figure at the end of the hallway was a very young man in uniform. At the sound of their footsteps he looked up, alert even though it was still the middle of the night.

"ID and floor you're visiting?" he said.

They flashed him their FBI IDs. "We're going down to the morgue," Mulder explained.

The guard shook his head. "That area is currently off limits to anyone other than authorized medical personnel."

Mulder eyed him coldly. "On whose orders?"

"General McAddie's."

Mulder didn't miss a beat. "General McAddie is who requested our coming here. We were awakened at three A.M. and told to get down here immediately."

"I don't know anything about that." The young naval guard frowned, glancing at the clipboard on his desk.

"Well, call General McAddie." Mulder stared impatiently down the corridor.

"I don't have his number."

"They can patch you in through the switch-board."

The guard bit his lip, then picked up the phone and began flipping through a huge directory. Mulder registered outraged disbelief.

"You don't know the switchboard number?"

"I'm calling my C.O.—"

Mulder reached over and disconnected the phone. He glared at the guard.

"Listen, son, we don't have time to mess around here, watching you demonstrate your ignorance in the chain of command. The order came direct from General McAddie. Call *him*. We'll conduct our business while you confirm authorization."

Without looking back, Mulder steered Scully past the security desk. Behind them the guard picked up the phone again.

"Why don't you go on ahead down, and I'll confirm authorization," he called after them.

Mulder nodded curtly. "Thank you."

They walked briskly down the corridor, only relaxing when they'd turned the corner into another hallway.

"Why is a morgue suddenly off limits on orders of a general?"

"Guess we'll find out," Scully replied, and pointed to the entrance to the morgue.

Inside they were met by a blast of frigid air. There were numerous gurneys, each holding a body beneath a white sheet. Scully made her way quickly down first one row and then another. She read IDs and dangling clipboards until she found what she was looking for.

"This is one of the firemen who died in Dallas?" she asked.

Mulder nodded. "According to this tag."

"And you're looking for?"

"Cause of death."

"I can tell you that without even looking at him," said Scully. "Concussive organ failure due to proximal exposure to source and flying debris—"

She pulled out the autopsy chart. "This body has already been autopsied, Mulder," she explained patiently. "You can tell from the way it's been wrapped and dressed."

Mulder worked to remove the sheet from the body. The first thing they saw was that it was still in its fireman's uniform. One sleeve lay empty alongside the torso, and where the chest had been the uniform sank until it grazed the bottom of the gurney.

"Does this fit the description you just read me, Scully?" Mulder asked.

"Oh my God. This man's tissue —" Scully pulled on a pair of latex gloves. She gently touched the man's chest. "It's—it's like *jelly*. There's some kind of cellular breakdown. It's completely edematous."

Her hands expertly checked for bruises, burns. Anything she might normally have found on a bombing victim. "Mulder, there's been no autopsy performed. There's no Y incision here; no internal exam."

Mulder picked up the autopsy report and shook it. "You're telling me the cause of death on this report is false. That this man *didn't* die from an explosion, or from flying debris."

"I don't know *what* killed this man. I'm not sure if anybody else could claim to, either."

"I want to bring him into the lab," said Mulder. "I'd like for you to examine him more closely, Scully."

She nodded. Together they pushed the gurney out of the freezer, and through the swinging doors that opened onto the pathology lab. Mulder pushed it over to the wall. Scully flipped the lights on and joined Mulder beside the gurney.

She said, "You knew this man didn't die at the bomb site before we got here."

"I'd been told as much."

"You're saying the bombing was a cover-up. Of what?"

"I don't know," admitted Mulder. "But I have a hunch that what you're going to find here isn't anything that can be easily explained."

Scully waited to hear if there was going to be more in the way of an explanation. When there wasn't, she tugged at one latex glove and sighed. "Mulder, this is going to take some time, and *somebody's* going to figure out soon enough that we're not even supposed to *be* here. I'm in serious violation of medical ethics."

Mulder pointed at the body on the gurney. "We're being *blamed* for these deaths, Scully. I want to know what this man died of. Don't you?"

She stared at him, then back down at the body. Finally she turned to the tray table set up on the wall behind them, the rows of sterilized scalpels and scissors and tweezers and knives that lay there, waiting. In silence she began gathering what she would need to do her job.

DUPONT CIRCLE, WASHINGTON, D.C.

Connecticut Avenue was nearly empty when Mulder climbed out of his cab and crossed it, stepping between stacks of plastic garbage bags heaped onto the curb. He started down R Street and saw two police cruisers pulled up in front of a brick row house. He glanced at the address scrawled on the paper in his hand, started up the walk, and went inside.

In the main room several uniformed officers milled about. In the adjoining office a police detective contemplated stacks of what appeared to be medical journals. He looked up as Mulder's shadow fell across the doorway.

"Is this Dr. Kurtzweil's residence?"

The detective eyed him suspiciously. "You got some kind of business with him?"

"I'm looking for him."

"Looking for him for what?"

Mulder pulled out his ID and flashed it at him. The detective glanced at it, then looked up and called to his partners in the next room, "Hey, the Feds are looking for him, too."

Mulder stepped into the middle of the small office, staring at the bookshelf. On each book the same name appeared in big letters.

DR. ALVIN KURTZWEIL

Mulder withdrew one of the books.

THE FOUR HORSEMEN OF THE GLOBAL DOMINATION CONSPIRACY

He glanced at it, then replaced it on the shelf.

"You want a call if we turn up Kurtzweil?" the detective asked.

Mulder started back for the door. "No. Don't bother."

Outside Mulder exited the apartment building, hoping it wouldn't take too long to find a cab. He'd only gone a few feet when he noticed a lanky silhouette gesturing furtively at him. It was Kurtzweil. When he saw that Mulder had noticed him he nodded, then stepped into the small space between two buildings. Mulder hurried after him.

Kurtzweil huddled up against the brick wall and shook his head furiously.

"What did I tell you?" he said. "Cloak and dagger stuff . . . Somebody knows I'm talking to you."

Mulder shrugged. "Not according to the men in blue. They seem to think you're a criminal of some sort."

"What is it this time? Malpractice?" Kurtzweil spat. "I've had my license taken away in three states."

Mulder nodded. "They want to discredit you— for what?"

"For what? Because I'm a dangerous man! Because I know too much about the truth . . ."

"You mean that end-of-the-world, apocalyptic garbage you write?"

A spark flared in Kurtzweil's eyes. "You know my work?" he asked hopefully.

Mulder took a deep breath. "Dr. Kurtzweil, I don't believe in any of that stuff."

Kurtzweil grinned. "I don't either, but it sure sells books."

Disgusted, Mulder headed out. Before he reached the sidewalk Kurtzweil collared him.

"I was right about Dallas, wasn't I, Agent Mulder?"

Mulder sighed. "How?"

"I picked up the historical document of the hypocrisy of the American government. The daily newspaper."

Impatience flickered across Mulder's face. "You said the firemen and the boy were found in the temporary offices of the Federal Emergency Management Agency. Why?"

Kurtzweil glanced nervously down the alley. "According to the newspaper, FEMA had been called out to manage an outbreak of the Hanta virus. Are you familiar with the Hanta virus, Agent Mulder?"

"It was a deadly virus spread by deer mice in the Southwest U.S. several years ago."

"And are you familiar with FEMA? What the Federal Emergency Management Agency's *real* power is?"

Mulder raised his eyebrows, waiting to hear how this was all going to fit. Kurtzweil went on, "FEMA allows the White House to suspend constitutional government upon declaration of a national emergency. It allows the creation of a non-elected government. Think about that, Agent Mulder."

Mulder thought. Kurtzweil's voice rose slightly, knowing he finally had an audience. "What is an agency with such broad, sweeping power doing managing a small viral outbreak in suburban Texas?"

"Are you saying," Mulder said slowly, "that it *wasn't* a small outbreak?"

Kurtzweil looked positively feverish. "I'm saying it wasn't the Hanta virus."

"What *was* it?" hissed Mulder.

"When we were young men in the military, your father and I were recruited for a project. They told us it was biological warfare. A virus. There were . . . rumors . . . about its origins."

Mulder shook his head. "What killed those men?"

"What killed them I won't even write about," Kurtzweil exploded. "I tell you, they'd do more than just harass me. They have the future to protect."

Mulder regarded him coolly. "I'll know soon enough."

But Kurtzweil was too worked up to hear him. "What killed those men can't be identified in simple medical terms," he went on. "My God, we can't even wrap our minds around something as obvious as HIV! We have no *context* for what killed those men, or any appreciation of the scale in which it will be unleashed in the future. Of how it will be transmitted; of the environmental factors involved . . ."

"A plague?"

"The plague to end all plagues, Agent Mulder," whispered Kurtzweil. "A silent weapon for a quiet war. The systematic release of an indiscriminate organism for which the men who bring it on still have no cure. They've been working on this for *fifty years*—"

He punched the air for emphasis. "—while the rest of the world was fighting commies, these men have been secretly negotiating a planned Armageddon."

Mulder frowned. "Negotiating with *whom?*"

"I think you know." Kurtzweil's mouth grew tight. "The timetable has been set. It will happen on a holiday, when people are away from their homes. When our elected officials are at their resorts or out of the country. The President will declare a state of emergency, at which time all federal agencies, *all* government, will come under the power of the Federal Emergency Management Agency.

"FEMA, Agent Mulder. The secret government."

Mulder whistled. "And they tell me *I'm* paranoid."

"Something's gone wrong—something unanticipated. Go back to Dallas and dig, Agent Mulder. Or we're only going to find out like the rest of the country—when it's too late."

BETHESDA NAVAL HOSPITAL

Scully was so involved with her autopsy that she almost didn't hear the click of a door opening. She yanked the sheet back over the fireman's corpse, darted to the freezer and slipped inside. Faint voices rose in the next room. She held her breath, listening.

"... *said they had clearance from General Mc-Addie* ..."

Suddenly her cell phone rang. She grabbed it and hit the ON button.

"Scully ... ?" She crouched behind the door, terrified the guard was about to burst in. "Scully?"

"Yeah?" she answered in a hoarse whisper.

"Why are you whispering?" She could hear the sounds of traffic; he was at a pay phone.

"I can't really talk right now," she said.

"What did you find?"

She took a breath. "Evidence of a massive infection."

"What kind of infection?"

"I don't know."

"Scully. Listen to me. I'm going home, then I'm booking a flight to Dallas. I'm getting you a ticket, too."

"*Mulder*—"

"I need you there with me," he went on quickly. "I need your expertise on this. The bomb we found was meant to destroy those bodies and whatever they were infected by."

She shook her head. "I've got a hearing tomorrow—"

"I'll have you back for it, Scully, I promise. Maybe with evidence that could blow your hearing away."

"Mulder, I can't," Scully's voice rose. "I'm already *way* past the point of common sense here—"

Loud voices sounded from the other side of the door. Without a "good-bye," Scully punched the phone off and shoved it into a pocket. Then she slid across the floor, ducking beneath one of the gurneys.

The door to the freezer opened. From where she

was hidden Scully could see the guard's shoes pass within inches of her face. Two other pairs of feet followed, as the guards crossed the freezer room, their steps echoing loudly on the linoleum floor. Scully's entire body began to shake. She gritted her teeth, the gurney's metal shelf pressing against her back like a blade.

At the far wall the guards hesitated. Scully watched as first one and then another stood on tiptoe. There was the bang of a steel cabinet being opened and closed; then the guards turned and went back to the door, the naval guard behind them. He had just passed the gurney where she huddled when abruptly he stopped. Scully held her breath, heart pounding; she could have grabbed him by the ankle if she wanted to.

Go, she thought, and closed her eyes. Go, *leave, just go . . .*

They left. The freezer's heavy doors slammed shut. Scully sighed, and waited until it was safe to follow.

CHAPTER 7

"You're looking for what amounts to a needle in a haystack." The field agent waved his hand to indicate the room around them, an open space the size of a basketball court. "I'm afraid the explosion was so devastating there hasn't been a whole lot we've been able to put together just yet."

Mulder had to agree. He raised an eyebrow, then turned back to the field agent.

"I'm looking for anything out of the ordinary. Maybe something from the FEMA offices where the bodies were found."

The field agent nodded. "We weren't expecting to find those remains, of course. They went right off

65

to Washington."

Mulder looked away, hoping his frustration and disappointment wouldn't show. "Was there anything in those offices that didn't go to D.C.?"

The field agent gestured at a table. "Some bone fragments came up in the sift this morning." He picked up a bottle and gazed at its contents. "We thought there'd been another fatality, but then we found out that FEMA had recovered them from an archaeological site out of town."

"Have you examined them?"

"No." The field agent shrugged. "Just fossils, as far as we know."

Mulder nodded, and a figure standing in the doorway caught his eye. He turned to the field agent and said, "I'd like this person to take a look, if you don't mind."

Scully waited in the doorway and stared at Mulder. The field agent acknowledged her with a nod of greeting.

"Let me just see if I can lay my hands on what you're looking for," he said.

Mulder gave Scully a puzzled look. "You said you weren't coming."

"I wasn't planning on it," she said coolly. "Particularly after spending a half hour in cold storage this morning. But I got a better look at the blood and tissue samples I took from the fireman."

"What did you find?"

Scully lowered her voice. "Something I couldn't show to anyone else. Not without more information. And not without causing the kind of attention I'd just as soon avoid right now."

She took a deep breath, and said, "The virus those men were infected with contains a protein code I've never seen before. What it did to them, it did extremely fast. And unlike the AIDS virus or any other aggressive strain, it survives very nicely *outside* the body."

Mulder's voice was a near whisper. "How was it contracted?"

"That I don't know."

At that moment the field agent reappeared. He carried a wooden tray holding several cork-topped glass vials. "Like I said, these are fossils," he announced. "And they weren't near the blast center, so they aren't going to help you much."

"May I?" Scully picked up the tray. One by one she held the vials up to the light. They held bone fragments. She selected one vial and stepped over to the chair beside a microscope. Very carefully she tapped out a tiny fragment onto the viewing bed. She leaned forward, adjusting the focus until it came into view.

Almost immediately she looked back up at

Mulder. He took in her expression and quickly turned to the field agent. "You said you knew the location of the archaeological site where these were found?"

The agent nodded. "Show you right on a map," he drawled. "C'mon."

BLACKWOOD, TEXAS

The midday sun beat down upon domed white tents rising like huge, dust-stained eggs amid the unmanned trucks surrounding them. Several large generators gave forth a muted hum, but otherwise the scene was completely desolate.

Within the central tent things were busier. At the edge of an earthen hole, a small bulldozer wrestled with a large Lucite container, maneuvering it until it was a few yards from the opening. Monitors and gauges covered every inch of the container's surface, along with oxygen tanks and something resembling a refrigeration unit. It looked more like the sort of thing you'd find on a lunar landing module than in the Texas flatlands.

And that's exactly what it was: a self-contained life-support system, its interior glazed with a thin, sugary layer of frost.

The bulldozer's engine cut off. Several technicians

appeared. They lined up alongside the machine's shovel and lifted off the container, carrying it gingerly toward the hole. As they did so, a flap at the end of the room opened and Dr. Bronschweig appeared, clad in his Haz-Mat suit, hood unzipped so that it hung across his shoulders. He waved at the technicians and started down the ladder into the hole.

"I need to have those settings checked and reset," he called, pointing at the container. "I need a *steady* minus two Celsius through the transfer of the body, after I administer the vaccine. Got that? *Minus two.*"

The technicians nodded. They set the container down and began checking gauges. Bronschweig disappeared down the hole.

Below, in the ice cave, it was dark save for the arctic blue glow coming from the plastic-draped area at one end of the chamber. Dr. Bronschweig walked across the cave, moved aside the plastic drapery, and entered.

He gasped.

The body of the fireman looked as though it had exploded. Where the inner organs had been was empty, as though whatever had been inside had eaten them. The gurney was smeared with red and the remains of gnawed bone and tissue.

"It's gone!" he shouted as he ran back to the ladder. *"It's gone!"*

"It's *what?*"

Overhead, the face of one of the technicians appeared.

"It's left the body," Dr. Bronschweig cried. Other technicians crowded around the first as Bronschweig began climbing the ladder. "I think it's hatched—"

He froze. "Wait," he said in a hoarse whisper. "I see it—"

In the shadows, something moved. Bronschweig held his breath, waiting. A moment later it appeared. It moved tentatively, almost timidly; like something newly born.

"Holy cow," whispered Bronschweig. His eyes widened in nervous wonder as he stared. He took a step back down to the ground. "So much for little green men . . ."

"You see it?" a technician called anxiously.

"Yeah. It's . . . amazing." He looked up at the faces ringed around the entrance to the cavern. "You want to get down here—"

Shakily he began working at the needle, trying to fit the syringe and the plunger in place. He glanced back at the shadows where the creature was, and—

It was gone. Bronschweig turned, scanning the cavern for where it might have fled. There was nothing. His hand tightened on the syringe as though it were a pistol—and then he saw it in the shadows across the cave. He stared at it for a split second, paralyzed, as its hands lifted and long pointed claws extended. It lunged at him, and they struggled violently.

Screaming, he stabbed the thing with the syringe before it threw him across the length of the cave. Terrified, Bronschweig staggered to his feet and made his way to the foot of the ladder. Blood trickled from a wound at his neck, but most of the damage seemed to have come to his suit.

"Hey," he cried brokenly, staring up the ladder into the technicians' stunned faces. "I need help . . ."

He glanced behind him, searching for signs of the creature; then back up the ladder. "*HEY*—What are you doing?"

They were closing the hatch. Shoving it down as fast as they could and frantically screwing the locks into place, even as Bronschweig watched in disbelief. He screamed but his screams went unheard. Above him there was a dull roar, and a dark blur floated across the transparent cover. The bulldozer's shovel rose and fell, and with each blow dumped another load of earth onto the hatch.

They were burying him alive.

In stunned silence he stood there; then from behind him there came a muffled sound—and it was on him, pulling him down, pulling him off the ladder and down into the darkness of the cave.

CHAPTER 8

SOMERSET, ENGLAND

Rovingsmere Mansion is one of those stately homes beloved of the English aristocracy. The man who stood at the conservatory window was a member of that elite group—and of another, more secret, world. Right now he stood at the window and watched as his grandchildren romped across an impeccably manicured lawn.

"Sir?"

He turned to see his valet holding open the conservatory door.

"Sir, you have a call."

For a moment the man remained. Finally he headed toward his study. He picked up the phone, positioning himself by the window so he could continue to watch his grandchildren. "Yes," he said.

From the other end of the line came a familiar voice, raspy from cigarette smoke. "We have a situation. The members are assembling."

The Well-Manicured Man winced. "Is it an emergency?"

"Yes. A meeting is set, tonight in London. We must determine a course."

The Well-Manicured Man's face tightened. "Who called this meeting?"

"Strughold." At the sound of this name the Well-Manicured Man nodded grimly. There could be no further questions. The voice on the phone continued. "He's just gotten on a plane in Tunis."

Without replying, the Well-Manicured Man dropped the phone back into its cradle. A child was screaming. He rushed to the window.

On the lawn beneath him, chaos had broken out. People were running to where the children had gathered silently around a fallen figure. A boy, his youngest grandchild. The valet knelt beside him, gently stroking the boy's forehead and calling out orders to the others. As the valet tenderly lifted the child into his arms, the Well-Manicured Man raced from the study, all thoughts of Strughold momentarily banished.

• • •

He did not arrive in London until shortly after eight that night. His limousine left him off in front of an anonymous building, and he went inside.

"Has Strughold arrived?" the Well-Manicured Man asked a valet who had met his car.

The valet indicated a long, dimly lit hallway. "They're waiting in the library, sir."

Inside, a group of men stood staring at a TV monitor. A black-and-white video was playing, dark forms moving jerkily across a darker background. As he entered, the men turned expectantly.

The Well-Manicured Man surveyed the group before joining them. Faces no one would recognize, though a word from one of them might bring a government crashing to its knees. Men who remained in the shadows.

In the center of the group stood a small, lean man with close-cropped hair, at once elegant and imposing. His gaze met the newcomer's, holding it for a moment too long. The Well-Manicured Man felt a shiver of unease.

"We began to worry," Strughold said. "Some of us have traveled so far, and you are the last to arrive."

"I'm sorry." The Well-Manicured Man looked at Strughold. "My grandson fell and broke his leg."

The other man went on, "While we've been made to wait, we've watched surveillance tapes which have raised more concerns."

"More concerns than what?" he asked.

"We've been forced to reassess our role in Colonization," explained Strughold. "Some new facts of biology have presented themselves."

"The virus has mutated," another voice broke in.

The Well-Manicured Man looked taken aback. "On its own?"

"We don't know." The Cigarette-Smoking Man put down the remote. "So far, there's only the isolated case in Dallas."

"Its effect on the host has changed," said Strughold. "The virus no longer just invades the brain as a controlling organism. It's developed a way to modify the host body."

The Well-Manicured Man's mouth grew taut. "Into what?"

"A new extraterrestrial biological entity."

The Well-Manicured Man stared at Strughold in disbelief. "My God . . ."

Strughold nodded. "The geometry of mass infection presents certain conceptual re-evaluations for us. About our place in their Colonization . . ."

"This isn't about Colonization!" the Well-Manicured Man exploded. "It's spontaneous repopulation! All our work . . ."

His voice trailed off. "If it's true, then they've been using us all along. We've been laboring under a lie!"

"It could be an isolated case," one of the others offered.

"How can we *know*?"

Strughold's voice rang out calmly. "We're going to tell them what we've found. What we've learned. By turning over a body infected with the gestating organism."

"In hope of *what*? Learning that it's true?" The Well-Manicured Man stared furiously at Strughold. "That we are nothing more than digestives for the creation of a new race of alien life forms!"

"Let me remind you who is the new race. And who is the old," Strughold responded coolly. "What would be gained by withholding anything from them? By pretending ignorance? If this signals that Colonization has already begun, then our knowledge may forestall it."

"And if it doesn't?" retorted the Well-Manicured Man. "By cooperating now we're but beggars to our own demise! Our ignorance lay in cooperating with the Colonists at all."

Strughold shrugged. "Cooperation is our only chance of saving ourselves."

Beside him the Cigarette-Smoking Man nodded. "They still need us to carry out their preparations."

"We'll continue to use them as they do us," said Strughold. "If only to play for more time. To continue work on our vaccine."

"Our vaccine may have no effect!" cried the Well-Manicured Man.

"Well, without a cure for the virus, we're nothing more than digestives anyway."

All eyes turned to see how the Well-Manicured Man would react to this. He was well respected by the members of the Syndicate. If his was now the lone voice crying in the wilderness, they would still hear him out.

"My lateness might as well have been absence," he said in barely restrained fury. "A course has already been taken."

"There are complications," said the Cigarette-Smoking Man. "Mulder saw one of the bodies that was destroyed in Dallas. He's gone back there again. Someone has tipped him off."

"Who?"

"Kurtzweil, we think."

"We've allowed this man his freedoms," interrupted Strughold. "His books have actually helped us to facilitate plausible denial. Has he outlived his usefulness to us?"

"No one believes Kurtzweil or his books," said the Well-Manicured Man impatiently. "He's a toiler. A crank."

"Mulder believes him," someone else said.

"Then Kurtzweil must be removed," said the Cigarette-Smoking Man.

"As must Mulder," pronounced Strughold.

The Well-Manicured Man shook his head angrily. "Kill Mulder and we risk turning one man's quest into a crusade."

"We've discredited Agent Mulder," said Strughold. "Taken away his reputation. Who mourns the death of a broken man?"

The Well-Manicured Man replied, "Mulder is far from broken."

"Then you must take away what he holds most valuable," said Strughold. He turned to stare at the monitor, where a woman's face now took up most of the screen. "The one thing in the world that he can't live without."

CHAPTER 9

BLACKWOOD, TEXAS

"I don't know, Mulder..." Scully shook her head, squinting into the glaring sunlight. In front of her a children's playground rose from the otherwise barren earth. "He didn't mention a *park*."

Mulder paced from the swings to the jungle gym to the slide. Everything brand-spanking new. The grass underfoot seemed new as well, thick and green.

"This is where he marked on the geological survey map, Scully." He jabbed at the folded paper in his hand. "Where he said those fossils were unearthed."

Scully made a helpless gesture. "I don't see any evidence of an archaeological dig, or any other kind of site. Not even a sewer or a storm drain."

Mulder scanned the area, confounded. In the distance the Dallas skyline shimmered in the heat, and children rode bikes in front of a modest housing development. He went back over to Scully, and together they walked around the edges of the playground.

"You're sure the fossils you looked at showed the same signs of deterioration you saw in the fireman's body in the morgue?"

Scully nodded. "The bone was porous, as if the virus or the causative microbe were decomposing it."

"And you've never seen anything like that?"

"No. It didn't show up on any of the immuno-histochemical tests—"

Mulder listened, staring down at his feet. Suddenly he stooped and ran his hand lightly over the tips of bright green there.

"This look like new grass to you?" he asked.

Scully tipped her head. "It looks pretty green for this climate."

Mulder knelt and dug his fingers into the thick carpet of turf. After a minute, he lifted up a corner. Under this the hard-baked surface of Texas dirt could be seen, brick-red and tough as sandstone.

"Ground's dry about an inch down," Mulder announced. "Somebody just laid this down. Very recently, I'd say."

Scully looked at the brightly painted swings and seesaws. "All the equipment is brand-new."

"But there's no irrigation system. Somebody's covering their tracks."

From behind them came the whizzing of bikes. Scully and Mulder turned. Four boys were riding near their rental car. When Mulder whistled loudly at them, they stopped and stared blankly at him.

"Hey," called Mulder, as he and Scully approached.

"Do you live around here?" asked Scully.

The boys exchanged looks. Finally one of them, Jason, shrugged and said, "Yeah."

Mulder stopped and regarded them. Pretty standard-issue middle America boys in buzzcuts and T-shirts. Two straddled brand-new BMX bikes. "You see anybody digging around here?"

The boys remained silent, until Chuck replied sullenly, "Not supposed to talk about it."

"You're not supposed to talk about it?" Scully prodded him gently. "Who told you that?"

Jeremy piped up. "Nobody."

"Nobody, huh? The same Nobody who put this park in? All that nice new equipment . . ."

Mulder gestured at the swing sets, then looked sternly down into the boys' guilty faces. "They buy you those bikes, too?"

The boys shifted uncomfortably. "I think you better tell us," said Scully.

"We don't even know you," Jason sniffed.

"Well, we're FBI agents."

Jason looked at Scully disdainfully. "*You're* not FBI agents."

Mulder suppressed a smile. "How do you know?"

"You look like door-to-door salesmen."

Mulder and Scully pulled out their badges. The boys' mouths dropped.

"They all left twenty minutes ago," Jeremy said quickly. "Going that way—"

They all pointed in the same direction.

"Thanks, guys," Mulder called. He pulled Scully after him and hurried toward the car.

The boys stood, silent, and watched as their rental car spun out onto the highway.

SOMEWHERE IN TEXAS

Mulder hunched at the wheel, foot to the floor. The car raced on, passing few other vehicles. Beside him Scully pored over the map.

"Unmarked tanker trucks . . ." Mulder said as if to himself. "What are archaeologists hauling out in tanker trucks?"

"I don't know, Mulder."

"And where are they *going* with it?"

"That's the first question to answer, if we're going to find them."

They drove on. It had been an hour since they'd seen another car. Mulder eased his foot from the accelerator, and let the car roll to a stop. In front of them was an intersection. Each road seemed to go absolutely nowhere: Nowhere North or Nowhere South.

For several minutes the car sat idling. Finally Mulder spoke, rubbing his eyes.

"What are my choices?"

Scully frowned. "About a hundred miles of nothing in each direction."

"Where would they be going?"

"We've got two choices. One of them wrong."

Mulder stared out his window. "You think they went left?"

Scully shook her head. "I don't know why—I think they went right."

A few more minutes of silence passed. Then Mulder pounded his foot on the gas. The car arrowed straight ahead onto the unpaved dirt road. Scully stared at him, waiting for an explanation, but he refused to meet her gaze.

Ahead of them the sun disappeared. Red and black clouds streaked the darkening sky, and a few stars pricked into view. Twenty minutes passed before Mulder finally spoke.

"Five years together," he said. "How many times have I been wrong?"

A few quiet seconds passed. "Never." He paused again. "At least not about driving."

Scully stared out at the night and said nothing.

Hours went by. Outside the night sky glittered, nothing but stars as far as you could see; nothing at all. When the car began to slow Scully felt as though she were being awakened from a dream. She turned reluctantly from her window to gaze at what was before them.

A few feet in front of the car, a line of barbed wire fences stretched endlessly. There was no gate, and as far as Scully could see, no break in the fence.

She opened the door and got out. Scully stared at a sign nailed to a post. Behind her, Mulder's door opened and he stepped out to join her.

"Hey, I was right about the bomb, wasn't I?" he asked plaintively.

"This is great," said Scully. "This is fitting."

She cocked her thumb at the sign.

SOME HAVE TRIED, SOME HAVE DIED.
TURN BACK—NO TRESPASSING.

"What?" demanded Mulder.

"I've got to be in Washington D.C., in eleven hours for a hearing—the outcome of which might possibly affect one of the biggest decisions of my life. And here I am standing out in the middle of Nowhere, Texas, *chasing phantom tanker trucks.*"

"We're not chasing trucks," Mulder said hotly, "we're chasing *evidence.*"

"Of *what*, exactly?"

"That bomb in Dallas was *allowed* to go off, to hide bodies infected with a virus. A virus you detected yourself, Scully."

"They haul gas in tanker trucks, they haul oil in tanker trucks—they don't haul *viruses* in tanker trucks."

Mulder stared stubbornly into the darkness. "Yeah, well, they may in this one."

"What do you mean by that?" For the first time Scully stared directly at him, her face clouded with anger and a growing suspicion. "What are you not telling me here?"

"This virus—" He turned away from her, afraid to go on.

"*Mulder*—"

"It may be extraterrestrial."

A moment passed while Scully gazed at him in disbelief. Then, "I don't believe this. I don't *believe* this!" she exploded. "You know, I've *been* here—I've been here one too many times with you, Mulder."

He kicked at a stone and looked at her, all innocence. "Been where?"

"Pounding down some dirt road in the middle of the night! Chasing some elusive truth on a dim hope, only to find myself *right* where I am right now, at *another* dead end —"

Her voice was abruptly cut off by the clanging of a bell. Blinding light strobed across their faces. Stunned, they whirled to stare at the barbed-wire fence.

In the sudden burst of light, a railroad crossing sign appeared to hang in the empty air. No swinging metal arms or gate; just that sign, an eerie warning in the wilderness. Mulder and Scully stared at it open-mouthed, then turned to gaze at a light growing upon the horizon. It grew larger and larger, until it became the headlamp on a train, speeding toward them.

And saw then what they had been chasing through the wasteland: two unmarked white tanker trucks, loaded piggyback on the flatbed cars. In seconds it was gone, swallowed by the night.

Mulder and Scully dashed madly back into their car. Mulder swung the car into a hard turn, and the engine roared as they took off after the train.

They followed it for a long time. In the distance

mountains loomed dead-black against a sky starting to fade to dawn. Except for the twin lines of the rails, there was no sign that any human had ever set foot here.

Then, very slowly, the tracks began to follow a long sloping upward grade. At last they could go no farther; the railroad tracks disappeared into the mountain, with not the slightest hint of what might lie on the other side of the tunnel. The car came to a stop at the edge of a gorge. Scully and Mulder clambered out, pulling on their jackets against the chill. In the near distance a strange glow stained the sky.

"What do you think it is?" Scully asked in a low voice.

Mulder shook his head. "I have no idea."

They started toward it, stumbling as they climbed down the hillside. At the bottom they could see what was illuminating the night: two gigantic, glowing white domes. Rolling to a stop beside them was the train that bore the unmarked tanker trucks.

Mulder pointed. Scully nodded, and without speaking they continued down. Finally they reached bottom. Ahead of them stretched the high desert plateau. They moved more quickly now, just short of running as they made their way across the wasteland. In the near distance something shimmered and rustled in the cold wind. But it wasn't until they were nearly upon it that the eerie glow from the domes revealed what lay before them.

"*Look*," breathed Scully in disbelief.

In the half light stretched acres and acres of corn fields. Wind rippled through the stalks, and Mulder and Scully walked until they stood at the edge of the field.

They entered the field. Scully shook her head. "This is weird, Mulder."

"Very weird."

"Any thoughts on why anybody'd be growing corn in the middle of the desert?"

Mulder pointed at the domes. "Not unless those are giant Jiffy Pop poppers out there."

At last they reached the end of the field. In front of them, bigger than they could have imagined, were the two glowing domes. There was no evidence that anyone was guarding them. For a moment the two agents stood staring at the eerie structures. Then they hurried cautiously toward the nearer of the two.

A heavy steel door served as entrance. Mulder pulled it and it opened with a sucking sound, suggesting that the interior was pressurized. He shot Scully a curious look, then stepped inside, Scully at his heels.

Immediately they both jumped. Overhead, large fans sent blasts of air down onto them.

"Cool in here," said Scully, shivering. She blinked; the interior of the dome was painfully bright. "Temperature's being regulated . . ."

"For the purpose of *what?*"

Mulder stared directly overhead. A dizzying web of cables was strung there. When he looked down he saw a floor that was gray and flat, utterly featureless. All around them the air was still, but as the two agents moved cautiously, they became aware of a sound. A hum, an almost electrical sound.

They headed toward the middle, stepping with care on the gray surface underfoot. Finally they reached the very center of the dome.

Before them, laid out in a grid, was row after row of what looked like boxes. Each was about three feet square. Mulder stepped very carefully onto one. It felt reassuringly solid, and after a moment Scully followed him, walking across the grid.

"I think we're on top of something, a large structure," Scully said. She stared down, frowning. The boxes had tops that could open, but right now these were all firmly shut. "I think these are some kind of venting—"

Mulder stooped to rest his head against the top of another box, listening. "You hear that?"

"I hear a humming. Like electricity. High voltage, maybe." She gazed overhead at the interior of the dome.

"Maybe," said Mulder. "Maybe not."

Scully pointed skyward. "What do you think *those* are for?"

Above them, at the very top of the dome, were two huge vents.

"I don't know," said Mulder.

They stood side by side, gazing at the ceiling, when without warning a hollow metallic *bang* echoed through the dome.

In the dome's ceiling one of the vents was opening. When the first vent was completely open, the second began the same ominous performance, sliding until it gaped onto the night. Mulder stared at it, mind racing as he tried to come up with some explanation for what was above them.

Cooling vents? But the dome was already chilly. Brow furrowed, he looked down and around, searching for something that might provide a clue. His gaze stopped when it came to the mysterious boxes underfoot.

Something occurred to him then. Something extremely unpleasant. Something frightening.

"Scully . . . ?"

His partner continued to stare upward. "Yeah . . . ?"

"Scully, listen to me."

"You've got about fourteen minutes to get this building evacuated."

"We're under pressure to give an accurate picture of what happened in the Dallas explosion to the Attorney General."

"If they want someone to blame, they can blame me. Agent Scully doesn't deserve this."

"I think that just about does it, Spooky."

"It's left the body. I think it's gestated—"

"Help! I nee

've been forced to reassess our role in Colonization."

"This is weird, Mulder. Any thoughts on why anybody would be growing corn in the middle of the desert?"

"Not unless those are giant Jiffy Pop poppers out there."

"You found something?"
"Yes. On the Texas border. Some kind of experiment."

"Find Agent Scully."

"Only then will you realize the scope and grandeur of the Project."

"Breathe!"

"Can you *breathe?*"

"Come on . . . it's time to go."

"One man alone cannot fight the future."

He grabbed her hand and pulled her after him. *"Run!"*

She hesitated and looked back at the gray boxes on the floor; and saw what they were hiding.

One by one the vents on each box opened, domino-style, sliding until their contents were exposed. With a sound like a chain saw ripping through new wood, bees emerged: hundreds of thousands of them, pouring from the boxes and streaming toward the open ceiling. Scully drew her hands before her face and turned, staggering after Mulder. He pulled his jacket up around his head and she did the same. The insects swarmed around her.

"Keep going!" Mulder shouted, voice muffled by his sleeve. Scully lurched after him. The entrance was only a few yards away now, but she was falling behind, losing her bearings as the swarm descended around her.

He was nearing the entryway when he turned to see Scully flagging behind him. She looked dazed and terrified.

"Scully!"

Mulder took a deep breath and raced back to her side. He grabbed her coat, heedless of the bees crawling there. Then he dragged her after him.

He kicked the door open and shoved her outside. He asked her if she got stung. "I don't think so," Scully said.

Before they could catch their breath something else came through the darkness. Not bees this time, but two blinding lights. The rushing whir of turbine engines filled the air as two unmarked helicopters came roaring from behind the other dome. They skimmed above the ground, searchlights blazing, headed right for Scully and Mulder.

The agents bolted out of sight just as the helicopters blasted over the spot where they had stood seconds before. They headed for the corn fields. Directly overhead the choppers swooped, searchlights cutting through the cornrows like twin lasers. Mulder and Scully ran in and out of the rows, barely managing to avoid the beams. The helicopters crisscrossed the air above them, banking sharply as they searched the fields below. The wash from their propeller blades ripped through the cornstalks like a tornado, revealing anything that might be hidden within.

In the field Mulder drew up beneath a broken cornstalk and looked around for Scully. She was gone. He stumbled back into the row, shielding his eyes as he peered between the endless lines of corn.

"*Mulder!*"

She was somewhere ahead of him. Mulder crashed through the field, gasping when he saw one of the choppers hovering into view. "*Scully!*" he yelled. *"Scully!"* He kept calling her name as he ran. The chopper hung in the air for a moment as though considering which way to go; then swung around and bore down upon him.

His heart pounded as he made a final effort, racing toward open ground. Behind him the chopper roared, cornstalks crashing in its wake. Mulder reached the end of the field and stumbled out into the night. He saw Scully a few feet away.

"Scully?" he called.

"Mulder," she said, sprinting toward him. "Let's *go*—"

They broke into a run, racing side by side toward the hillside that hid their car. When they reached the hill, they climbed frantically. It was only when they reached the summit that they slowed and looked at each other in the darkness.

It was ominously quiet. The helicopters had disappeared.

"Where'd they go?" Scully coughed, wiping her eyes.

"I don't know." Mulder stood for a moment, surveying the weirdly glowing domes and acres of corn. Then he turned and continued running, back to the bluff where their car was parked. Scully followed. They jumped inside, Mulder twisting the ignition and pounding on the gas.

It didn't start.

"Oh no," he groaned.

"Mulder!" cried Scully.

From behind the bluff rose one of the black helicopters. It hovered above them. Suddenly the car's engine roared to life. Mulder threw it into gear and spun out, tires screaming as he turned the car and sent it churning back down the hillside without turning on the lights. Scully stared back breathlessly, waiting for the helicopter to give chase.

It did not. It hovered for a few seconds, then, as silently as it had appeared, it banked and flew off into the night.

 **CHAPTER 10**

Assistant Director Jana Cassidy did *not* like to be kept waiting. She sighed impatiently and looked at her watch, then up again as the door swung open.

Assistant Director Walter Skinner stuck his head in. "She's coming," he said wearily.

He withdrew to let Scully pass. She had on the same clothes she'd been wearing for two days now. Skinner came in behind her and joined the others at the table.

"Special Agent Scully," Cassidy began, reshuffling her papers.

"I apologize for making you wait," Scully broke in. "But I've brought some new evidence with me—"

"Evidence of what?" Cassidy asked sharply. Scully reached into her satchel and pulled out a vinyl evidence bag.

"These are fossilized bone fragments I've been able to study, gathered from the bomb site in Dallas . . ."

Cassidy looked at her coolly. She didn't notice the other thing Scully had brought back with her from Texas. Beneath the young agent's mass of red hair a bee crawled, as though stretching its legs from the long journey.

"You've been back to Dallas?"

Scully nodded. "Yes."

"Are you going to let us in on *what*, exactly, you're trying to prove?"

"That the bombing in Dallas may have been arranged to destroy the bodies of those firemen, so that their deaths and the reason for them wouldn't have to be explained—"

Unnoticed, the bee disappeared from sight again beneath the collar of Scully's suit jacket.

Cassidy's eyes narrowed. "Those are very serious allegations, Agent Scully."

Scully stared at her hands. "Yes, I know."

Cassidy leaned back and regarded Scully. "And

you have conclusive evidence of this? Something to tie this claim of yours to the crime?"

"Nothing completely conclusive," Scully admitted grudgingly. "But I hope to. We're working to develop this evidence—"

"Working with?"

Scully hesitated. "Agent Mulder."

Jana Cassidy looked at Scully, then indicated the door.

"Will you wait outside for a moment, Agent Scully? We need to discuss this matter."

Very slowly Scully stood. She picked up her satchel and walked to the door, glancing back in time to see the look Walter Skinner gave her, a look compounded equally of sympathy and disappointment.

CASEY'S BAR,
WASHINGTON, D.C.

It was late afternoon when Fox Mulder pushed open the door to Casey's. He made his way to the back of the room, where a lone figure was slumped in a high-backed wooden booth. When Mulder sat down next to him the man jumped, then quickly leaned over to grab the agent's hand.

"You found something?" Kurtzweil wheezed.

"Yes. On the Texas border. Some kind of experiment. Something they excavated was brought there in tanker trucks."

"What?"

"I'm not sure. A virus—"

"You saw this experiment?" Kurtzweil broke in excitedly.

Mulder nodded. "Yes. But we were chased off."

"What did it look like?"

"There were bees. And corn crops." Kurtzweil stared at him, then laughed with nervous delight. Mulder opened his hands in a helpless gesture. "What *are* they?" he asked.

The doctor slid from his seat. "What do you think?"

Mulder looked thoughtful. "A transportation system," he said at last. "Transgenic crops. The pollen genetically altered to carry a virus."

"That would be my guess."

"Your *guess?*" Mulder exploded. "You mean you didn't *know?*"

Kurtzweil didn't reply. Without looking back he headed for the back of the bar. Mulder gaped, then hurried after him.

He caught up with Kurtzweil near the bathrooms. "What do you mean, your *guess?*"

Kurtzweil said nothing and continued to head for the back door. Mulder collared him, yanking the older man so that the two were inches apart.

"You told me *you had the answers*."

Kurtzweil shrugged. "Yeah, well, I don't have them all."

"You've been *using* me—"

"*I've* been using *you?*" Now it was Kurtzweil's turn to sound offended.

"You didn't know my father—"

The doctor shook his head. "I told you—he and I were old friends—"

"You're a liar," Mulder spat. "You lied to me to gather information for you. For your stupid books. Didn't you?" He shoved the older man against the bathroom door. "Didn't you?"

Suddenly the door swung open. A man hastily exited, making his way between them. As he did so Kurtzweil broke away and hurried out the back door. Mulder quickly followed.

"Kurtzweil!"

When he came up alongside Kurtzweil, the older man turned on him with unexpected ferocity.

"You'd be out of luck if not for me," he gasped, pushing at Mulder's chest. "You saw what you saw because *I led you to it*. I'm putting my butt on the line for you."

"Are you kidding?" Mulder's voice crackled with disdain. "I just got chased across Texas by two black helicopters—"

"And why do you think it is that you're standing here talking to me? These people don't make mistakes, Agent Mulder."

Kurtzweil spun on his heel and strode off. Mulder gazed at him, dumbfounded by the logic of this, when his attention was shaken by a noise above him. He whirled and looked up to see a figure straddling a fire escape. A tall man, only his legs and feet clearly in sight, but it was obvious he had been watching them. As Mulder moved back to get a better view the man turned and stared down at him, then ducked into an open window and disappeared.

It was only a glimpse, but something about the figure was familiar. His height, the close-cropped black hair . . .

Mulder frowned and hurried down the alley after Kurtzweil.

He was gone. Mulder chugged onto the sidewalk, scanning the street and surrounding buildings. Kurtzweil was nowhere to be seen. Finally he had to admit it: Kurtzweil had given him the slip.

When he reached his apartment Mulder hurried inside, forgetting to close the door behind him. He crossed quickly to his desk, yanking open drawers until he discovered a stack of photo albums. He opened them, glancing at the Polaroids and faded photos and dropping them on the floor.

Until he found it. An album filled with page after page of photos taken during his Wonder Years. His sister Samantha's fifth birthday party. Fox and Samantha on the first day of school. Fox and Samantha and their mother. Samantha with their dog.

And there, alongside pictures of his parents and cousins he hadn't seen in decades, a family barbecue. His mother kneeling on the lawn between Fox and Samantha, their father at the grill, smiling. At his side stood a tall man with dark hair, smiling, not stooped at all and much younger.

Alvin Kurtzweil.

A knock shattered his reverie. Mulder looked up to see Scully standing in the open door of his apartment.

"What?" He got to his feet, scattering photos around him. "Scully? What's wrong?"

"Salt Lake City, Utah," she said softly. "Transfer effective immediately."

He shook his head.

"I already gave Skinner my letter of resignation," she added brokenly.

Mulder stared at her. "You can't quit, Scully."

"I can, Mulder. I debated whether or not to even tell you in person, because I knew—"

He took a step toward her and gestured at the photos at his feet. "We're close to something here," he said. "We're on the verge—"

"*You're* on the verge, Mulder." She blinked, teary-eyed, and looked away. "Please—please don't do this to me—"

He continued to gaze at her. "After what you saw last night," he said at last. "After all you've seen, Scully—You can't just walk away."

"I have. I did. It's done."

He shook his head, stunned. "Just like that . . ."

"I'm contacting the state board Monday to file my medical reinstatement papers —"

"But I *need* you on this, Scully!" he said urgently.

"You don't, Mulder. You've never needed me. I've only held you back." She turned and started for the door. "I've got to go."

He caught her before she reached the elevator. "You're wrong," he cried.

Scully turned on him. "*Why* was I assigned to you?" she asked fiercely. "To *debunk your work*. To rein you in. To shut you down."

He shook his head. "No. You've saved me, Scully." He put his hands lightly on her shoulders and gazed down into her blue eyes. "As difficult and frustrating as it's been sometimes, your strict rationalism and science have saved me—a hundred times, a *thousand* times. You've—you've kept me honest and made me whole. I owe you so much, Scully, and you owe me nothing."

He dipped his head and went on in a voice barely above a whisper. "I don't want to do this without you. I don't know if I can. And if I quit now, they win . . ."

He gazed down at her and she stared back at him. She moved very slightly away from him. His hands remained barely touching her arms as she lifted herself on tiptoe and kissed his forehead.

He did not move away. Their eyes met and linked. A sudden inexplicable tension flared. And then his hands tightened on her, he drew her toward him. For an instant she hesitated, then reached for him. She could feel his mouth grazing hers, when—

"Ouch!" Scully pulled away from Mulder, rubbing her neck.

"I'm sorry." Mulder stared at her, worried he had done something wrong.

Scully's voice was thick. "I think . . . something . . . stung me."

He gasped as Scully slumped forward, and caught her in his arms. Her head lolled drunkenly as Mulder whispered, frightened, "Scully . . . ?"

She stared up at him and opened her hand. In the

palm lay a bumblebee. "Something's wrong," she murmured, barely coherent. "I'm having . . . lancinating pain . . . my chest. My . . . motor functions are being affected. I'm—"

As gently as he could, Mulder lowered her until she lay upon the floor. She continued to speak, her voice growing fainter and fainter, eyes no longer focusing.

". . . my pulse feels thready and I—I've got a funny taste in the back of my throat."

Mulder strained to hear. "I think you're in anaphylactic shock—"

"No—it's—"

"Scully . . ."

"I've got no allergy," she whispered. "Something . . . this . . . Mulder . . . I think . . . I think you should call an ambulance . . ."

He raced for the phone, punching in 911. "This is Special Agent Fox Mulder. I have an emergency. I have an agent down—"

Minutes passed before he heard sirens wailing outside. He ignored the elevator and ran downstairs, holding the door open as two paramedics rushed past him. When they reached Scully, one paramedic opened the stretcher while the other knelt beside her.

"Can you hear me?" he said in a loud voice. "Can you say your name?"

Scully's lips moved but no words came out. The paramedic shot a look at his partner. "She's got constriction in the throat and larynx." He looked back down at her and asked, "Are you breathing okay?"

No reply. He lay his head beside her mouth, listening. "Passages are open. Let's get her in the van."

They bundled her onto the stretcher and Mulder went with them outside to where the EMT van waited, lights flashing.

"She said she had a taste in the back of her throat," he said. "But there was no pre-existing allergy to beestings. The bee that stung her may have been carrying a virus—"

The second paramedic stared at him. "A virus?"

"Get on the radio," the first medic shouted at the van driver. "Tell them we have a cytogenic reaction, we need an advise and administer—"

They guided the stretcher to the back of the vehicle, lifting it in with expert hands. Scully's eyes rolled and then focused on Mulder. The paramedics quickly moved into the van. Before Mulder could climb aboard and join Scully the paramedics swung the doors closed.

"Hey—what hospital are you taking her to?" he said as the doors were closing.

He ran to the driver's side of the van, waving frantically. Mulder knocked on the window.

"What hospital are you taking her to?"

He got his first look at the driver, a tall man in a light blue EMT uniform, his hair close-cropped. He stared coldly out at Mulder, who drew up short beside the door.

Because suddenly, in a split second, it all fell together. It was the uniform that triggered his memory: the tall man on the fire escape, sliding into an open window; the tall man in a vendor's uniform exiting the snack room where the bomb had been. And now the driver of the van . . .

It was the same man. His hand was raised, aiming a handgun directly at Mulder. The next instant a blast echoed through the night. Mulder fell backward, clutching his head as the ambulance shrieked away. He lay bleeding in the street and his neighbors watched, horrified, as a second ambulance roared up, skidding to a halt to let two other paramedics leap out and rush to the fallen man's side.

NATIONAL AIRPORT,
WASHINGTON, D.C.

An hour later an unmarked truck sat on the runway at National Airport. A private jet taxied slowly toward it. The truck's engines cut off. Two men in black fatigues hopped down and swiftly moved to the rear of the vehicle. Carefully they removed a large container covered with monitors and gauges, oxygen tanks and refrigeration units. Inside lay Scully. She was so still she might have been dead, except that as the men carried the container from the truck, her eyes moved very slightly.

The jet rolled toward the truck. When it was perhaps twenty feet away, it halted. A door on the plane opened. Steps unfolded down to the runway, and a moment later a man appeared. He stood at the top of the stairs, watching, then withdrew a pack of cigarettes and lit one. He stood smoking, as the men loaded the container into the cargo hold.

When they were finished the men turned and hurried back to the truck. The Cigarette-Smoking Man reboarded the aircraft. The plane swung around and headed for the central runway. Ten minutes later its lights could be seen arcing through the night above the city.

CHAPTER 11

INTENSIVE CARE UNIT,
GEORGE WASHINGTON UNIVERSITY HOSPITAL

"I think he's coming out . . ."

"He is—he's coming to!"

"Hey, Mulder . . ."

In his bed, Mulder blinked painfully. It hurt to even think about opening his eyes, so for a long time he didn't; only lay there listening to the voices above him. Men's voices, incredibly, *annoyingly*, familiar.

"Mulder . . . ?"

He opened his eyes. Above him were three faces.

"Oh no . . ." Mulder moaned.

Langly shook his head, his long hair falling in his face. "What's wrong?"

Beside him Frohike and Byers gazed at the agent in concern.

"Tin Man," Mulder whispered in amazement, staring first at Byers, then Langly. "Scarecrow—"

He raised his head slightly, indicating Frohike. "—Toto." He sat up, rubbing his face and frowning at the bandage he found. "What am I doing here?"

"You were shot in the head," Byers explained. "The bullet broke the flesh on your right brow and glanced off your temporal plate."

Mulder ran a finger over the bandage. "Penetration but not perforation," he said.

Langly nodded. "Three centimeters to the left and we'd all be playing harps."

"They gave you a craniotomy to relieve the pressure from a subdural hematoma," Byers went on. "But you've been unconscious since they brought you in."

"Your guy Skinner's been with you around the clock," said Frohike.

Langly broke in, "We got the news and made a trip to your apartment. Found a bug in your phone line—"

Byers dangled a minuscule microphone in front of Mulder's face.

"*And* one in your hall," Frohike added. He held up a small vial containing a bumblebee.

Mulder stared at it as his memory flooded back. "Scully had a violent reaction to a beesting—"

"Right," said Byers. "And you called 911. Except that call was intercepted."

Mulder shook his head. "They took her—"

He pushed the covers off, moving shakily as he tried to swing his legs to the ground. As he did so, the door to his room opened a bit. Assistant Director Walter Skinner peeked in, his expression changing from concern to surprise when he saw Mulder standing up.

"Agent Mulder!"

Mulder looked up, nearly losing his balance in the process. "Where's Scully?" he asked thickly. Langly grabbed his shoulder to keep him from falling.

Skinner came into the room. He crossed to Mulder's side and regarded him for a long moment before replying, "She's missing. We've been unable to locate her or the vehicle they took her in."

"Whoever they are—" Mulder's voice shook, and Langly tightened his hold on him protectively. "—this goes right back to Dallas. It goes right back to the bombing."

Skinner nodded. "I know." At Mulder's stunned look he went on, "Agent Scully reported your suspicions to OPR. On the basis of her report, I sent techs over to SAC Michaud's apartment. They picked up PETN residues on his personal effects—and analysis showed the residue was consistent with the construction of the vending machine device in Dallas."

Mulder sat back down on the bed. "How deep does this go?"

"I don't know."

For a minute Mulder just sat there, taking it all in. When he lifted his head again, he saw a figure framed in the small window of the room door. A man in a suit, casting a furtive glance in to where Mulder, Skinner, and the Lone Gunmen were gathered. The stranger stared at them, then hurried off. Mulder quickly turned back to Skinner.

"Are we being watched?"

"I'm not taking any chances."

Mulder nodded. He pulled at the bandage on his head and peeled it away, revealing the wound. He looked at one of the Lone Gunmen. "I need your clothes, Byers."

Byers started. "Me?"

Skinner frowned. "What are you doing, Agent Mulder?"

Already Mulder was shedding his hospital gown. "I've got to find Scully—"

"Do you know where she is?" asked Frohike.

"No." Mulder dropped his hospital gown and motioned anxiously at Byers. "But I know someone who might have an answer . . .

"Who better," he ended with grim determination, as reluctantly Byers began to remove his clothes.

A short while later the door to Mulder's room opened. First Langly then Frohike stepped out into the corridor, glancing around nervously as behind him a second figure appeared, clad in Byers's clothing. Standing a few feet away, his back to them, a man in a suit leaned against the wall. As they started down the hall, the man in the suit looked up. He glanced at them, then casually turned and drifted toward Mulder's room, his eyes revealing his suspicions as he peered through the little window.

Inside, tucked into the hospital bed with the sheets pulled up to his nose, a figure lay motionless. Beside him Walter Skinner stood talking on the phone. The man in the suit stared at the bed, frowning, then turned to look back down the hall again.

At the end of the corridor the three men walked quickly, Langly and Frohike flanking Mulder. As they rounded the corner Frohike passed him a cell phone. Without hesitation, Mulder punched in Dr. Kurtzweil's number.

CHAPTER 12

In the dark alley behind Casey's, Alvin Kurtzweil waited anxiously for Fox Mulder. When he saw no sign of him, he turned and started back for the door. He stepped inside, and came up short against a man in a cashmere overcoat, his hands raised in mock surprise.

"Dr. Kurtzweil, isn't it? Dr. *Alvin* Kurtzweil?"

Kurtzweil gasped. He tried to edge away, but the Well-Manicured Man only smiled.

"You're surprised. But certainly you've been expecting some response to your indiscretion . . ."

Kurtzweil shook his head. "I didn't tell him anything."

"I'm quite sure that whatever you told Agent Mulder, you have your good reasons," the other man said. "It's a weakness in men our age: the urge to confess." He paused, then added, "I have much to confess myself."

Kurtzweil stared at him, confused. Finally he blurted, "What are you doing here? What do you want from me?"

"I'd hoped to try and help you understand. What I'm here to do, is to try and protect my children. That's all. You and I have but short lives left. I can only hope that the same isn't true for them."

He waited and held the door open. Kurtzweil stood as though considering the other man's words. Then he suddenly bolted back into the alley. He had only gone a few paces when headlights blinded him. A car pulled into the alley. Kurtzweil stopped and turned to stare with terrified eyes at the man still standing calmly in the doorway.

Fox Mulder barreled through the front door of Casey's, looking frenziedly for Kurtzweil. Mulder made his way to the back, to the doctor's usual booth.

It was empty. Mulder turned and ran down the

dank hallway where the bathrooms were, and burst out into the alley.

A Town Car sat idling on the cobblestone pavement. Behind it a tall, beautifully dressed man and his uniformed driver were arranging something in the trunk. As Mulder stared, they closed the lid. The elegant man looked up, and said in greeting, "Mr. Mulder."

Mulder's hands clenched. "What happened to Kurtzweil?"

The Well-Manicured Man shrugged. "He's come and gone."

"Where's Scully?" demanded Mulder.

"I have answers for you."

"Is she alive?"

"Yes," the Well-Manicured Man said. "I'm quite prepared to tell you everything, though there isn't much you haven't already guessed."

Mulder took a step toward him. "I want to know where Scully is."

The Well-Manicured Man nodded. Mulder tensed as he reached into his jacket pocket, and removed a thin envelope of dark-green felt. The Well-Manicured Man said, "The location of Agent Scully. And the means to save her life. Please—"

He gestured toward the car, where the driver stood holding the back door open. Mulder hesitated, then moved past the Well-Manicured Man and slid into the seat. The older man got in after him and closed the door. The car pulled away.

Without a word the Well-Manicured Man handed Mulder the small felt envelope.

"What is it?" Mulder asked.

"A weak vaccine against the virus Agent Scully has been infected with. It must be administered within ninety-six hours."

"You're lying."

"No." The Well-Manicured Man stared out the tinted window. "Though I have no way to prove otherwise. The virus is extraterrestrial. We know very little about it, except that it is the original inhabitant of this planet."

Mulder looked dubious. "A *virus?*"

"A simple, unstoppable life form. What *is* a virus, but a colonizing force that cannot be defeated? Living in a cave underground, until it mutates. And attacks."

"*This* is what you've been trying to conceal?" Mulder no longer tried to keep the contempt from his voice. "A disease?"

"No!" exploded the Well-Manicured Man. "For God's sake, you've got it all *backward*—

"AIDS, the Ebola virus—on an evolutionary scale, they are newborns. *This* virus walked the planet long before the dinosaurs."

Mulder scowled. "What do you mean, 'walked'?"

"Your aliens, Agent Mulder. Your little green men—they arrived here millions of years ago. Those that didn't leave have been lying dormant underground since the last Ice Age, in the form of an evolved pathogen. Just waiting to be reconstituted when the alien race returns to colonize the planet. And using *us* as hosts. Against this we have no defense. Nothing but a weak vaccine . . ."

He paused and stared pointedly at Mulder, who finally looked shaken. "Do you see why it was kept secret, Agent Mulder? Why even the best men—men like your father—could not let the truth be known? Until Dallas, we believed the virus would simply control us. That mass infection would make us a slave race."

"That's why you bombed the building," said Mulder slowly. "The infected firemen . . . the boy . . ."

The Well-Manicured Man nodded grimly. "Imagine our surprise when they began to hatch. My group has been working cooperatively with the alien colonists, facilitating programs like the one you saw. To gain access to the virus, in hope that we might secretly develop a cure."

"To save yourselves," broke in Mulder.

The Well-Manicured Man shrugged. "When war is futile, victory consists of merely staying alive.

Survival is the ultimate ideology." He hesitated. "Your father wisely refused to believe this."

"My father sacrificed my sister!" cried Mulder angrily. "He let them take Samantha—"

"No." For a moment the Well-Manicured Man looked almost sorrowful. "Without a vaccination, the only true survivors of the viral holocaust would be those immune to it: human/alien clones. He *allowed* your sister to be abducted, to be taken to a cloning program. For one reason."

"So she'd survive," Mulder breathed in sudden understanding. "As a genetic hybrid . . ."

The Well-Manicured Man nodded. "Your father chose hope over selfishness. Hope in the only future he had: his children. His hope for you, Agent Mulder, was that you would uncover the truth about the Project. That you would do everything you could to stop it—

"That you would fight the future."

He fell silent. On the other side of the car seat, Mulder sat, stunned; feeling as though all at once his destiny had been validated, or maybe simply justified. "Why are you telling me this?" he said at last.

The Well-Manicured Man stared at his hands for a long time before replying. "For the sake of my own children. Nothing more, nothing less. Once they learn what I've told you, my life will be over."

He raised his head, and Mulder looked up to see the driver staring back at them from the rearview mirror. At their notice he quickly brought his attention back to the road, and Mulder asked, "What happened to Dr. Kurtzweil?"

"His knowledge became too great for his indiscretion. As your father knew, some things need to be sacrificed to the future."

Mulder stared at the other man's impassive face and suddenly realized the truth of it.

"You—you *murdered* him—" Mulder said in shocked disbelief. When the Well-Manicured Man said nothing, Mulder grabbed his door handle. "Let me out. Stop the car."

The Well-Manicured Man gestured at the front seat. "Driver . . ."

Slowly the limo pulled to a stop. Outside the street was empty. Mulder jimmied the handle. It was locked. He whirled to challenge his captor, and found himself looking down at a handgun. Its barrel was aimed directly at Mulder's chest.

"The men I work with will stop at nothing to clear the way for what they believe is their stake in the inevitable future," the Well-Manicured Man said. "I was ordered to kill Dr. Kurtzweil."

Mulder backed against the door as the other man lifted the gun. "—as I was ordered to kill you."

But before Mulder could cry out, the Well-Manicured man whirled and shot the driver in the head.

Blood spattered the front windshield. Mulder gasped, trying to comprehend what had just happened, and stared horrified at the man holding the gun beside him. "Trust no one, Mr. Mulder," said the Well-Manicured Man matter-of-factly. Mulder looked at him, expecting to be next. But the Well-Manicured Man only opened the door and stepped from the car.

"Get out of the car, Agent Mulder."

"Why? The upholstery is already ruined."

"Get out."

Taking a deep breath, Mulder joined him. He looked down at the felt envelope in his hand.

"You have precious little time, Agent Mulder. What I've given you—the alien colonists don't know it exists . . . yet.

"I need to know *how*—" Mulder cried.

"The vaccine you hold is the only defense against the virus. Its introduction into the alien environment may have the power to destroy the delicate plans we've so assiduously protected for the last fifty years."

"May?" Mulder clutched the envelope and shook his head. "What do you mean, may?"

"Find Agent Scully. Only then will you realize the

scope and grandeur of the Project. And why *you* must save her. Because only her science can save you."

Mulder stared at him, waiting for more. But the Well-Manicured Man only pointed down the street. "Go."

Mulder started to protest, but the other man raised the gun and pointed it at him.

"Go *now!*"

Mulder went. Behind him the Well-Manicured Man stood watching him for a moment; then turned and got back into the car. He shut the door, and Mulder had the faintest glimpse of movement behind the tinted glass. Seconds later, the car exploded.

The impact wave knocked Mulder to the ground. He lost his grasp on the precious envelope and it briefly flew from his hand into the darkness. Gasping he struggled to his feet, and reached out for the little dark-green rectangle. Its contents spilled on the street. The light from the blazing car touched what was there: a syringe; a small glass ampule, miraculously undamaged; and a tiny piece of paper with numbers written on it.

BASE 1
SOUTH 83° 00 LAT.
EAST 63° 00 LONG.
326 FEET

Mulder picked up the envelope and its contents. Then he began to run, as behind him the first wails of police sirens and fire engines echoed through the night.

CHAPTER 13

POLE OF INACCESIBILITY,
ANTARCTICA, 48 HOURS LATER

The ice was so vast and colorless that it blended into the sky. There was only white: endless, eternal, terrible. Inside the cab of the snow tractor, Mulder's breath turned to vapor. He hunched over the controls, focusing all of his energy on what lay before him. The tractor crawled like an insect across the Ross Ice Shelf.

Hours passed. Finally he maneuvered the tractor to a stop, reached for the handheld Global Positioning Satellite monitor to check his position. He squinted as numbers scrolled across the GPS monitor's screen, then stared hard out the front window. He glanced down at the GPS device one more time, then stepped outside.

Snow crunched underfoot, snow whirled around his head. He trudged across the ice. When he looked back at the snow tractor it looked very small and insubstantial against the endless white ground and steely sky. He began a long ascent of a gentle slope, now and then sliding and catching himself by digging hands or heels into the soft new snow. When he reached the top he dropped to his knees.

Spread out across the plain below was an ice station, surrounded by tractors and Sno-Cats and snowmobiles. Mulder pulled a pair of compact high-powered binoculars from his parka and scanned the domes and support vehicles, looking for signs of life. None, until he let his sight linger on the most distant dome.

There, jolting over the ice fields, was another snow tractor. It crept toward the ice station, coming to a halt beside one of the domes. A door opened on the dome and a man emerged, wearing a parka and a fur hat. He stood on the doorstep for a moment, his face obscured by a cloud of vapor. Then he tossed something into the snow and walked to the vehicle.

The Cigarette-Smoking Man. Mulder watched as he yanked on the door of the snow tractor and climbed inside. The vehicle reversed, then slowly crawled off toward the far horizon.

Mulder drew the binoculars back from his eyes. He stumbled to his feet and started toward the ice station.

He moved cautiously, weighing each step before setting foot on the ice crust before him. Mulder's gaze remained fixed on the domes. He had only a few hundred yards left to go when beneath one boot the ice crust gave way. There was an instant when the world seemed to tremble. Then the ground collapsed.

He fell, landing on his back. The surface beneath him was cold and hard and smooth. He lay there for a moment, trying to determine if he'd broken anything. Pain shot through one arm, and the gun wound at his temple throbbed, but after a minute he rolled over.

He had fallen on some hard, narrow, metallic structure. There was a vent in the floor through which air blew. Mulder pulled off the hood of his parka and his gloves, and looked deep into the vent, then back up at the hole he'd fallen through. No way back up there, and nothing around him but solid ice. He gazed back at the vent.

It was his only choice. He took a deep breath, then pulled himself forward into the darkness.

Inside was cold and pitch-black. He moved cautiously, feeling ahead of him. The corridor snaked downward until a pinprick of light appeared. When he reached the end he squeezed through headfirst and swung himself down onto the ground.

Mulder blinked and shoved his hand into his pocket, fumbling until he withdrew a flashlight. It clicked on; he swept it up and down in front of him, revealing a terrifying landscape.

He stood in the middle of an endless corridor carved into the ice. To the left and right, as far as he could see, were tall glassy shapes, regularly spaced, like ice coffins stood upright against the walls. He pointed the light directly in front of him. Mulder reached to brush frost from the surface ice, and gasped at what he saw.

There was a man frozen in the ice. Naked, his eyes open and staring. His hair was long and dark and matted, his features oddly inhuman. Drawing closer Mulder could see that the man's flesh looked like that of the fireman in the morgue. Mulder drew back in revulsion as he saw something *inside* the man: an embryonic creature with huge black eyes, frozen like its host.

Mulder turned and paced down the ice corridor. Where it ended, dim light seeped through several low, arched openings. Mulder dropped to his knees to peer through, and saw before him a brief passage that widened into a sort of balcony. He bellied down and pulled himself through the arch. When he reached the other end, he poked his head out on to the balcony and gazed up in wonder.

All around him was space, sweeping to a domed ceiling high above him. He looked down; wherever the bottom was, it was at least as far away as the top. All around him, circling the dome, were countless other ports. He gazed down to the floor of the dome. Leading to it were several enormous tubes. One angled up past Mulder.

It took several minutes for all this to sink in. The scale was too immense, much huger than anything Mulder had ever seen. But strangest and most terrifying of all was what he saw: row upon row of man-sized pods, dark-colored, hanging from long railings that extended into the darkness. He squinted, trying to figure out what they were, and where the seemingly endless rows led. Hundreds of feet above Mulder, another figure gazed in disbelief at what was before him. Within the heated cab of his Sno-Cat, the Cigarette-Smoking Man leaned forward to clear a spot on the foggy windshield. At last he could see it clearly—

The snow tractor Mulder had left behind on the ice.

For a long moment, the Cigarette-Smoking Man stared at the tractor. Then, without a word, he turned his own vehicle, and as quickly as he could, he drove back to the base.

Beneath the ice, Mulder continued to watch the strange pods. He noticed that in the far side of the dome, the rows appeared to be moving. He blinked, trying to get a better view, and then saw what he had not noticed before.

On the floor hundreds of feet below him, lay a discarded cryolitter. Mulder tore his gaze away and looked at the long tubelike structure that rose a few feet behind him. Without stopping to think of the danger, Mulder swung himself over and slipped inside.

It was tight, but he could fit. He began to climb down, struggling to see in the near-darkness, hands and feet slipping on the oily walls. He climbed down for what seemed like hours, fighting exhaustion, when without warning his hands slipped and he began to slide. He struggled to stop, but continued until he reached the end of the tube and found himself striking a narrow ledge. He scrambled desperately, at last managing to hold on.

Gasping for breath, he looked down. As he did so the binoculars slipped from his pocket and fell. He watched them fall, and waited for the sound of their impact, waited and waited and then held his breath, to make sure he wouldn't miss the sound of them hitting bottom.

He heard nothing. He looked downward and saw an unimaginably black and bottomless pit. The sight terrified him. With every ounce of strength that remained, Mulder pulled himself along the ledge, his fingers digging into the slick material, until finally he managed to lift himself up, and then over, onto the inner side.

He took a deep breath, then got to his feet. He was in a sort of corridor, darker and warmer than the one he had left. He pulled out his flashlight and shined its beam on the tunnel. He saw the cryolitter and approached it hesitantly. Inside were Scully's clothes and the little gold cross she always wore around her neck. He stooped and picked up the cross, pocketed it, and walked on.

Throughout the entire length of the corridor, a metal rack was suspended from the ceiling. Hanging from the rack were the pods—the objects he had seen on the upper level. But here it was warm enough that they were not completely frozen. He walked along slowly, his flashlight tracing the outlines of what each cryopod held: a human body, barely visible behind a thin covering of green ice.

But the faces that stared out from these pods were not the primitive features of the things he had seen above. These were men and women like himself. Each had a tube in his or her mouth.

133

Mulder walked alongside the row, staring at first one face, then another. Trying not to admit to himself what he was looking for—*who* he was looking for—until he saw her.

"Oh, no," he whispered.

He stopped in front of a wall of green ice. There, within one of the frozen pods, was Scully. Her hair covered with snow, a look of horror on her face.

Mulder struck the cryopod with his flashlight, smashing it against the icy covering again and again: nothing. He remembered the cryolitter and he ran to it, grabbing one of the oxygen tanks from its lid and racing back to Scully. Grunting with effort, he raised the tank and drove it repeatedly against the cryopod.

With a crack the pod shattered. Ice and slush spilled onto the ground, and for the first time he saw Scully clearly. Her body was covered with frost. With shaking fingers he unzipped his jacket and felt for the envelope in the inner pocket. He pulled out the syringe and ampoule, wrestling with the rubber cap and squinting to see the needle in the darkness. Then he jabbed it into her shoulder.

Almost instantly, a thick amber liquid oozed from the tube in her mouth. Then the tube began to shrivel. At the same moment the tunnel shook. Mulder was thrown and nearly crashed into the wall.

He steadied himself, then yanked the tube from Scully's mouth.

Her eyes blinked, her lips moved as she tried to suck in air. Her eyes rolled, trying to focus, and still the air would not reach her lungs.

"Breathe!" Mulder cried. "Can you breathe?"

Before him she strained, her expression desperate, like a swimmer struggling to come up for air. Then amber liquid suddenly poured from her mouth. She began to cough and gag, taking huge gulps of air as her eyes finally focused on Mulder. Her mouth worked as she tried to speak.

"What?" Mulder leaned into her, putting his ear against her mouth.

"Cold—"

"Hang on," said Mulder grimly. "I'm going to get you out of here."

Inside the ice station the room began to shake. The Cigarette-Smoking Man hurried past rows of computers where men sat, their eyes fixed on the blinking screens. In front of one monitor, a man looked up worriedly as the Cigarette-Smoking Man hastened to his side.

The man pointed at the screen, where a complex

system of graphs had suddenly changed, numbers and levels skyrocketing. "We've got a contaminant in the system," he said.

The Cigarette-Smoking Man stared at the screen. "It's Mulder. He's got the vaccine."

Without another word he turned and hurried for the door. Around him men were running as they began evacuating the ice station. The Cigarette-Smoking Man ignored them and headed for his tractor. There he was met by a gaunt man whose close-cropped hair was almost hidden beneath his parka hood. It was the man who had shot Mulder. He flung open the door of the tractor and climbed inside.

"What's happened?" he yelled.

The Cigarette-Smoking Man swung into the cab. "It's all going to hell."

The snow tractor began to pull away. Behind them steam vents erupted on the surface. Beneath the ice station, hot air blasting from the ducts was causing the ice shelf to melt and collapse.

"What about Mulder?" the other man shouted.

The Cigarette-Smoking Man glanced behind them and shook his head. "He'll never make it."

The tractor began to pull away. Behind them, mist rose like smoke from the domed structures.

• • •

Hundreds of feet below, the narrow passages of the buried spaceship filled with fog. Mulder swung his flashlight before him, trying to pierce the mist with its weak beam. Scully was in his arms, her limp body held awkwardly in a fireman's carry. She wore Mulder's snow parka and nylon outer pants, and her face grazed his shoulder as she tried to lift her head to speak.

"We've got to keep moving," Mulder said hoarsely. All around them water streamed from the hanging cryopods. The entire structure vibrated as Mulder struggled on.

Approaching the place where Mulder first slipped down into the passage, the walls were now slick with running water. When they reached the end of the passage, they found the base of a tube and began to climb. At the top, they found themselves in the upper corridor where Mulder had first seen the prehistoric man.

Its body was no longer encased in solid ice. Through the layers of ice and translucent skin the creature inside could be seen, turning very slightly as though coming awake. Mulder gazed at it, then quickly turned and stared up at the ceiling.

"Scully, reach up and grab that vent."

She did not respond. He looked down and saw that she had lost consciousness. With gentle urgency he laid her on the floor. "Scully, come on, Scully—"

He unzipped her jacket, his fingers moving across her neck as he sought a pulse. "Scully—"

She strained harder to breathe as he thrust his fingers into her mouth, clearing her passageway. "Breathe, Scully." He pumped her chest, forcing air into her.

One. Two. Three.

He leaned down and put his mouth against hers, feeling how cold her lips were, and her cheeks. He breathed into her, turning his head away and listening for the sound of air in her lungs.

Nothing.

He pumped her chest again, his movements growing more and more frantic.

One. Two. Three.

Behind him, unseen, the creatures thrashed within their hosts, as the ice around them began to fall in chunks to the floor. At the sound, Mulder turned and saw them trying to escape. He continued CPR, ignoring everything but Scully.

Then beneath him she suddenly moved. She sucked in air, and then began to cough. She gazed at Mulder, eyes focusing on his, and her lips parted.

"Mulder—" she said in a pained whisper. "Mulder—

"Had you big time."

The faintest grin flitted across his face. Before he could reply, a loud *chunk* echoed from behind him. Mulder whipped his head around.

"Oh, my God—"

Dark forms were moving in the corridor. Arms and legs thrust from the cryopods, as their three-fingered hands beat at the crumbling ice.

The creatures were beginning to hatch.

Mulder quickly turned to look the other way. The same scene greeted him: slush pouring from the pods as the creatures' powerful feet kicked holes in the icy pods. He turned back to his partner.

"Scully! Reach up and grab that vent—"

Her mouth moved but no words came out. With all his remaining strength Mulder lifted her, turning to where the vent opened in the wall above them. He propped her against his shoulder and pushed her toward the vent. She grabbed it and pulled herself up, disappearing through the opening. Behind her Mulder jumped and found a handhold, kicking at what was below. With a hoarse cry a creature burst free, grabbing at Mulder's foot. He kicked at it furiously as its claws slid down his legs. Just as it stumbled from its pod, Mulder yanked himself from its grip and swung himself up and into the vent.

Inside Scully moved feebly.

"Scully!" he shouted. "Keep going!"

She moaned in reply, but moved ahead.

"Keep going, Scully—"

They inched onward, Mulder pushing her when she no longer had to strength to continue. At last the vent opening was above them. Mulder pushed her through and followed, gasping at the bite of cold, fresh air. He looked back constantly to see if any of the creatures were following.

He and Scully were in the air pocket formed when Mulder had first fallen down from the ice shelf. All around them, the ice and snow were melting. Overhead a crater-sized hole had opened. Mulder got shakily to his feet. Again he looked back.

With an inhuman shriek, one of the creatures leaped from the vent opening, claws extending toward him. Before it could reach him, a blast a steam sent it hurling back down. There was a low rumble. More steam curled up from the vent. With a cry Mulder grabbed Scully by the shoulders. He threw her toward the far wall, leaping after her and covering his eyes.

Behind them, a volcanic blast of steam shot from the vent they had just left. Mulder grabbed Scully and stumbled toward the surface of the ice sheet.

They reached the top. Together they staggered away from the vent. They came to a small rise and climbed up it, falling often in the soft snow. When they got to its summit, they turned to look back.

Below them was the ice sheet. A series of regularly spaced holes had appeared in it, and through these steam was blasting, defining the circular craft beneath. The white domed tents now seemed tiny compared to the enormous structure under the surface. As they stared, steam from below blasted with terrible force, the sound so loud they covered their ears against it. Mulder grabbed Scully's sleeve and pulled her protectively toward him.

Suddenly the ice rippled, and without warning the entire sheet gave way. The ice station plunged downward, caving in to the very center of the buried ship. Shock waves radiated outward. The ground trembled as Mulder realized what was happening.

"We've got to run!"

He dragged her after him, the two of them looking back to see where the ice shelf was collapsing. Geysers were erupting everywhere, shooting hundreds of feet into the air. Mulder and Scully fled through a landscape of smoke and flying snow, dodging chunks of ice and burning debris. In the center of the collapsing shelf a black shape appeared. It grew more and more immense as they ran, struggling to outrace it.

With a cry Scully fell, arms flailing at the soft

snow. Mulder yanked her back to her feet, his ears numbed by the roar of the emerging spacecraft. He grabbed her hand, but before they could flee farther the ground beneath them fell away.

They fell, and fell, and finally landed, hard, on the flat surface of the ship. As it lifted into the air they slid off it and down, falling through the air until they crashed onto the ice sheet below. Ice chunks fell like rain all about them. Mulder crouched over Scully, trying to shield her from the deadly hail of debris, as the vast, black spacecraft continued to rise above them, so huge that it blotted out the sky. Faster and faster it rose, gaining momentum as it broke free of the frozen weight of the Antarctic ice. Scully moaned, her face pressed down into the snow. Above her, Mulder stared awestruck as the ship lifted clear of the earth, rotating slowly as it hovered in the sky. For the first time he could see it clearly, the network of spokes and cells that held it together and the smooth central dome.

It continued to rise, and now the craft began to glow as with some unimaginable heat. All around it the sky shimmered and pulsed, as the ship seemed to expand.

And then, with a last blinding, deafening burst of energy, it disappeared into the clouds. The spacecraft was gone.

Mulder stared at the empty sky, then at Scully.

Her eyes opened and she gazed back at him. Then, slowly as a child falling asleep, he lay his head down upon the snow. His body heaved with exhaustion; his eyes closed. Moments later he began to shiver, unconscious.

Next to him Scully lay, still as death. A freezing wind howled cross the waste. She began to cough. She fought to lift her head, blinking.

She looked at Mulder. His face was white and he was unconscious. With all the strength she had, she pulled him close to her, holding him against her body and warming him.

She gazed back over her shoulder, at the immense crater left by the ship, dwarfing the wasteland around them, two tiny figures invisible against the endless ice.

CHAPTER 14

"—in light of the report I've got here in front of me—in light of the narrative I'm now hearing—"

Assistant Director Jana Cassidy sat in the middle of the conference table, surrounded by her colleagues. At the end of the table sat Assistant Director Walter Skinner, his gaze flicking from Cassidy to the red-haired woman who sat at a smaller table in the center of the room, the chair beside her noticeably empty.

"—my official report is incomplete, pending these new facts that I'm being asked to reconcile. Agent Scully—"

Dana Scully tilted her head. Her face showed signs of minor frostbite, but otherwise was healed. As Cassidy spoke her blue eyes darkened with restrained defiance.

"—while there is direct evidence now that a federal agent may have been involved in the bombing, the other events you've laid down here seem too incredible on their own, and quite frankly, implausible in their connection."

"What is it you find incredible?" Scully asked.

Jana Cassidy suppressed a smile. "Well, where would you like me to start?"

As she spoke, a black-clad figure moved silently through the Dallas Field Office hundreds of miles away. A flashlight beam suddenly pricked through the darkness. The beam swung back and forth, revealing jars, shattered plastic, twisted bits of wreckage. At last it settled on a table set up with microscope and magnifying glass, where several small vials were nestled in a cardboard box.

The man holding the flashlight moved quickly, silently, to the table. He was tall and gaunt-faced, his hair close-cropped. When he reached the table he extended one gloved hand and picked up a vial, a tiny glass bottle containing fragments of petrified bone. The man glanced at the contents, then pocketed the evidence. As quickly and quietly as he had arrived, he disappeared, and the room was dark once more.

"—Antarctica is a long way from Dallas, Agent Scully," Jana Cassidy continued without a beat. "I can't very well submit a report to the Attorney General that alleges the links you've made here."

She picked up the file, then dropped it in front of her. "Bees and corn crops do not quite fall under the rubric of domestic terrorism."

Somewhere in the wilderness west of Dallas, a seemingly endless field of corn began to blaze as a group of men with flamethrowers began to walk slowly and purposefully along the rows.

In the FBI Office of Professional Review, Scully shook her head, once. "No, they don't."

"Most of what I find in here is lacking a coherent picture of any organization with an attributable motive—"

Cassidy paused and stared directly at Scully—the first sympathetic look she'd given her since the proceedings had begun. "I realize the ordeal you've endured has clearly affected you—though the holes in your account leave this panel with little choice but to delete these references from our final report to the Justice Department—"

In an anonymous cul-de-sac, three unmarked tanker trucks sat beneath the blazing sun. A man in dark clothes, wearing sunglasses, moved slowly alongside first one and then another of the trucks, painting bright yellow words and an ear of corn on the tanks: NATURE'S BEST CORN OIL.

"And until a time," Jana Cassidy finished smoothly, "when hard evidence becomes available that would give us cause to pursue such an investigation."

As Cassidy spoke, Scully's hand slipped into her coat pocket. When the assistant director grew silent, Scully stood and approached the conference table.

She removed something from her pocket and placed it in front of Jana Cassidy.

"I don't believe that the FBI currently *has* an investigative unit qualified to pursue the evidence at hand," said Scully.

Jana Cassidy frowned and picked up what the agent had set there: a tiny glass vial containing a dead bumblebee. She studied it as, without asking permission, without another word, Agent Scully headed for the exit.

As the door closed behind her, Cassidy furrowed her brow and turned to Walter Skinner. "Mr. Skinner?" she asked, and waited for his reply.

CONSTITUTION AVENUE,
WASHINGTON, D.C.,
NEAR FBI HEADQUARTERS

Fox Mulder sat on a park bench near the Mall, reading that morning's Washington Post. When he reached a small item in the national news his eyes widened.

FATAL HANTA VIRUS OUTBREAK
IN NORTHERN TEXAS
REPORTED CONTAINED

He looked up. A figure was approaching him. When it grew closer, he saw it was Scully.

He stood and handed her the newspaper. "There's a nice story on page twenty-seven. Somehow our names were left out."

Scully took the paper without looking at it. Mulder went on, "They're burying it, Scully. They're going to cover it all back up and no one will know."

Clearly upset, he spun on his heels and began to walk away. Scully followed him.

"You're wrong Mulder," she said. "I just told everything I know to OPR."

Mulder stopped and looked at her. "Everything you know?"

Scully nodded and they began to walk again. "What I experienced. The virus. How it's been spread by bees from pollen in transgenic corn crops—"

"And the flying saucer?" he broke in mockingly. "With the infected bodies and its little unscheduled departure from the polar ice cap?"

"I admit I'm still less than clear on that. On what exactly I saw. And its purpose."

Mulder turned to her. "It doesn't matter, Scully," he said. "They're not going to believe you. Why would they? If it can't be programmed, cataloged, or easily referenced—"

"I wouldn't be so sure, Mulder," said Scully.

Mulder's anger had turned to impatience. "How many times have we been here? Right here. Grasping at the unbelievable truth? You're right to leave. You should get away from me. As far as you can."

"You asked me to stay," Scully said challengingly.

"I said you didn't owe me anything," countered Mulder. "Especially not your life. Go be a doctor, Scully."

Scully shook her head. "I will. But I'm not going anywhere. This illness, whatever it is, has a cure. You held it in your hand—"

She took his hand and gazed up at him "—if I quit now, they win."

They stood without speaking. In the distance, the Cigarette-Smoking Man sat in a nondescript car, watching them. He took a last puff on his cigarette and flicked it onto the street. The car's electric window rolled up, and he drove off.

FOUM TATAOUINE, TUNISIA

Early morning heat shimmered above the rows of corn stretching endlessly toward the horizon. A man in traditional Arab garb led a second man in a dark suit through the green and golden stalks.

"Mister Strughold!" the Arab shouted. "Mister Strughold!"

Conrad Strughold emerged from the rows of corn. "You look hot and miserable," said Strughold. "Why have you traveled all this way?"

The Cigarette-Smoking Man stared at him coolly. "We have business to discuss."

"We have regular channels," said Strughold.

"This involves Mulder," said the Cigarette-Smoking Man.

Strughold winced. "Ah, that name! Again and again—"

"He's seen more than he should," said the Cigarette-Smoking Man.

Strughold made a dismissive gesture. "What has he seen? Of the whole, he has seen but pieces."

"He's determined now," insisted the Cigarette-Smoking Man. "Reinvested."

"He is but one man. One man alone cannot fight the future."

The Cigarette-Smoking Man held something out to Strughold. "Yesterday I received this—"

Strughold took it from his hand: a telegram. He read it, then stared at the horizon without actually seeing what was there. Then he dropped the telegram. In silence he turned and headed back toward the cornfield.

On the ground the telegram rustled slightly in the wind. The words showed stark black against yellow paper.

X-FILES RE-OPENED. STOP.
PLEASE ADVISE. STOP.

The wind rose, lifted the telegram and sent it spinning into the air. The telegram fluttered and swooped, rising higher and higher, until finally it disappeared into the sky. As far as the eye could see, row and rows of cornfields stretched. Acres of cornfields; miles. Extending across the Tunisian desert, where two immense white domes reared up against the horizon.